Contents

Cleaning agents

Cleaning agents are often poisonous, so keep well away from children. Only use bottles provided and label them carefully. They are often inflammable and sometimes give off toxic fumes. Some can burn the skin, so protect your hands when using them.

Never smoke whilst using or use near an open fire. **Always** open windows whilst using.

ABRASIVE CLEANERS: *Ajax, Vim* (powders); *Chemico, Gumption* (pastes); *Ajax Cream, Jif, Gumption Cream,* (liquids). From supermarkets. **Always** follow instructions.

ABRASIVE PAPER: Glasspaper/sandpaper, emery paper, wet and dry paper. From hardware stores.

ABSORBENT PADS: Cottonwool, *Kleenex*, paper napkins, soft white cloth.

ABSORBENT POWDERS: Fuller's earth, cat litter, sawdust (for hard surfaces). French chalk, powdered starch, talcum powder (for fabrics). All absorbent powders listed above are harmless to surfaces but may be difficult to remove from dark, non-washable fabrics.

ACETIC ACID: See White Vinegar.

ACETONE: From chemists. **Fabrics:** Harmless to most natural and synthetic fibres. **Never** use on acetate, triacetate, modacrylic and viscose (rayon). **Always** test first. Inflammable. Toxic fumes. See also Amyl Acetate.

ALL-PURPOSE CLEANERS: *Johnson's Sparkle, Mr Sheen* (Aerosol); *Jif, Handy Andy* (liquids); *Flash* (powder). From supermarkets. **Always** follow instructions.

AMMONIA (HOUSEHOLD): From supermarkets, hardware stores. **Always** follow instructions. **Fabrics: Never** use on silk, wool or their blends. Never use undiluted. Never let it dry on the fabric. **Always** rinse well after use. Always test first. Use white vinegar or lemon juice solution if ammonia affects colour. Use 1 tablespoon/15 ml to 1 pint/500 ml of water. Sponge or soak for about 3 minutes. Poisonous. Toxic fumes. If spilt on skin wash immediately, then apply vinegar or lemon juice.

AMYL ACETATE: From chemists. **Never** use on plastics. Inflammable. Toxic fumes. **Fabrics:** Use instead of acetone on acetate, triacetate, modacrylic and viscose (rayon). Non-oily nail varnish remover can also be used as a substitute. **Always** test first.

ART GUM ERASER: From artists' supply stores.

BATH CLEANER: *Jif, Cleen-o-Pine, Bathbrite, Flash, Izal Bath Cleaner, Gumption Cream* (for most surfaces); *Impact* (for plastic surfaces). From supermarkets. **Always** follow instructions.

BATH STAIN REMOVER: *Jenolite Bath Stain Remover.* From hardware stores. **Always** follow instructions.

BICARBONATE OF SODA: From chemists, grocery stores and supermarkets.

BLEACH: See Chlorine Bleach, Hydrogen Peroxide and Wood Bleach.

BORAX: From supermarkets. **Fabrics:** Harmless to most fibres. **Always** test first. Use 1 tablespoon/15 ml of domestic borax to 1 pint/500 ml warm water. Soak for about 10 minutes. Can be used directly on white fabrics.

CARPET SHAMPOO: *Bissell Foam Carpet Shampoo, 1001, Sabco Carpet & Upholstery Shampoo, Sapur Carpet Cleaner.* From department stores. **Always** follow instructions.

CARPET SPOTTING KIT: *Holloway's Carpet Care Spot Removing Kit.* **Always** follow instructions. From manufacturers (see p.33).

CERAMIC HOB CLEANER: *Corning* (conditioner and powder). From hardware stores or local LEB showroom.

CHLORINE BLEACH: *Brobat, Domestos, Parozone.* From supermarkets. Poisonous. Do not store in a metal container or use on or with metal objects. **Always** follow instructions. **Never** mix with other cleaning agents. **Fabrics: Never** use on silk, wool, mohair, leather, linen, viscose (rayon), elastane or on drip-dry or deep-coloured cottons, or on articles with flame-proof or crease-resistant finishes. Never use undiluted. Rather treat fabric a few times with a weak solution than once with a strong one. Use 1 tablespoon/15 ml liquid bleach to 1 pint/500 ml cold water. Sponge or soak for 5–15 minutes. Never leave for longer than half an hour. **Always** rinse well afterwards. Always follow instructions and test first.

CHROME CLEANER: *3 in 1 Chrome Cleaner.* From hardware stores. **Always** follow instructions.

COLOUR AND STAIN REMOVER: *Dygon.* From hardware stores.

CREAM OF TARTAR: From supermarkets.

DENTURE CLEANER: *Steradent.* From chemists.

DETERGENT POWDERS, AUTOMATIC: Biological – *Ariel, Bold, Daz, New System Persil, Surf, Tide, Bio-Tex* (soaker and prewasher). From supermarkets. **Fabrics: Never** use on protein fibres; wool or silk or non-colourfast, flame-resistant or rubberised fabrics. Never soak zips or other metal fastenings. **Always** test first. Always follow instructions. Non-biological – *Persil (original non-biological), Dreft Automatic.* From supermarkets. **Always** follow instructions. Use lather only on non-washable fabrics.

DETERGENTS, MILD: *Dreft, Fairy Snow, Lux Flakes, Stergene. Woolite* – for hand-washing colourfast woollens and other delicate items. From supermarkets. Milder than detergent powders. **Fabrics:** May be used directly on some stains.

DEVELOPER: From photographic stores. Use ½ teaspoon/2.5 ml hypo to ½ pint/250 ml warm water.

DISTILLED WATER: From chemists and motor accessory stores.

DRAIN CLEANER: *Simonez, Drainfree.* From supermarkets. **Always** follow instructions.

DRY-CLEANER: *Goddard's Dry Clean, Dabitoff Spray, K2r Aerosol* (aerosols); *Boots Dry Cleaner, Beaucaire, Liquid Dabitoff, Thawpit* (liquids); *K2r* (paste). From supermarkets. Inflammable. Toxic fumes. **Fabrics: Never** use on leather, suede, rubber, plastics or waterproofed fabrics. Never use in a washing machine. Rather treat fabrics several times with a weak solution than once with a strong one. Apply only to dry surfaces. **Always** follow instructions.

EUCALYPTUS OIL: From chemist. Use undiluted. May smell after and during use.

FLOOR POLISH: *Johnson Klear, Seel* (emulsion); *Novashield, Marley Floor Gloss, Mansion One Two, Mansion Wax, Mansion Guardshine, Ronuk, Johnson Original Paste Wax.* From supermarkets and hardware stores. **Always** follow instructions.

FURNITURE POLISH: *Stephenson's Olde English Furniture Cream, Topp's Teak Cream; Antiquax* (non-silicone); *Johnson Wax, Rentokil Wax Polish* (pastes); *Topp's Original, Liquid Gold, Favor* (aerosols). From supermarkets. *Kleeneze Antique Furniture Polish.* From the manufacturers (see p. 33). **Always** follow instructions.

FURNITURE RENOVATORS: From hardware stores. **Always** follow instructions.

GLASS/PLASTIC CLEANER: *Debby.* From hardware stores.

GLASS/WINDOW CLEANER: *Ajax Window Cleaner, 1001, Sparkle, Windolene.* From supermarkets. **Always** follow instructions.

GLYCERINE: From chemists. Safe to use on most fabrics. Use diluted in equal parts with warm water. Rub into fabric and leave for up to an hour to soften stain. Rinse well with warm water after use.

GLYCERINE SOAP: *Propert's Saddle Soap.* From department stores. **Always** follow instructions.

HYDROGEN PEROXIDE: From chemists. Buy 20 volume strength. See text for instructions. **Fabrics: Never** use on nylon or flame-resistant fabrics. **Always** test first. Use 1 part 20 volume peroxide to 4 parts cold water and add a few drops of ammonia. Never add ammonia if the fabric is silk or wool or contains silk or wool. Soak whites if necessary overnight; soak coloured 5–15 minutes.

IODINE: From chemists.
IRON (PRESSING) CLEANER: *Vilene Iron Cleaner.* From hardware stores. **Always** follow instructions.
JEWELLERY CLEANER: *Goddard's Jewellery Care.* From hardware stores.
KETTLE DE-SCALER: *Kay-Dee, Albright Scale Away, Kettle Fur Collector.* From hardware stores. **Always** follow instructions.
LAVATORY CLEANER: *Sanilav, Harpic, Jeyes Liquid.* From supermarkets. **Always** follow instructions. **Never** use with bleach.
LEATHER SHOE POLISH: *Wren, Cherry Blossom, Kiwi; Tuxan All-Purpose* (liquid), *Meltonian* (cream). From supermarkets. **Always** follow instructions.
LEATHER RENOVATOR: *Connolly's Cee Bee Hide Food* (for untreated leather only). From department stores. *British Museum Leather Dressing* (see p. 33). **Always** follow instructions.
LIGHTER FUEL (Petroleum Spirit): *Ronsonol.* From tobacconists. Inflammable. **Fabrics: Never** use on acetate, triacetate, modacrylic or viscose (rayon) fabrics. **Always** test first. Use undiluted.
LINSEED OIL: From art stores.
MALT VINEGAR: From supermarkets. Use neat or diluted with water.
MARBLE CLEANER: *Bell 1967 Cleaner.* From hardware stores (or see p. 33). **Always** follow instructions.
MELAMINE CLEANER: *Melfresh.* From hardware stores. **Always** follow instructions.
METAL POLISH: *Goddard's Long Term Brass and Copper Polish, Duraglit Wadding* (brass and copper); *Silvo, Quicksilva, Goddard's Silver Dip, Goddard's Long Term Silver Polish (silver); Silvo* (soft metals); *Bluebell, Brasso, Hi Sheen* (stainless steel); *Polaris* (hard metals). From hardware stores. **Always** follow instructions.
METHYLATED SPIRIT: From hardware stores. Inflammable. Poisonous. **Fabrics: Never** use on acetate, triacetate, modacrylic or viscose (rayon) fabrics. **Always** test first. Use neat.
NAIL VARNISH REMOVER (NON-OILY): From chemists. Inflammable. **Fabrics: Never** use on acetate, triacetate, modacrylic or viscose (rayon) fabrics. Use neat.
OIL STAIN REMOVER: *Jizer, Swarfega.* From hardware stores. **Always** follow instructions.
OVEN CLEANER: *Brillo Oven, Grill and Barbecue Cleaner, Shift* (aerosols); *Oven Pad; Kleenoff* (aerosol or paste). From supermarkets. **Always** follow instructions.
PAINT BRUSH CLEANER: *Polyclens Plus.* From hardware stores. Inflammable. **Always** follow instructions. **Fabrics: Never** use on acetate, triacetate, modacrylic or viscose (rayon) fabrics. **Always** test first.
PAINT REMOVER: *Polystrippa.* From hardware stores. **Always** follow instructions.
PAINTWORK CLEANER: *Flash, Jif, Mr Sheen, Sparkle, Mangers Sugar Soap.* From supermarkets. **Always** follow instructions.
PARAFFIN: From hardware stores. Poisonous and inflammable.
PENETRATING OIL: *3 in 1 Penetrating Oil.* From hardware stores. **Always** follow instructions.
PERSPEX CLEANER: *Perspex* Anti-static cleaner. From Perspex stockists. **Always** follow instructions.
PICTURE CLEANER: *Windsor & Newton Artists' Picture Cleaner.* From art stores. **Always** follow instructions. **Never** use on valuable paintings.
PRE-WASH AEROSOLS: *Frend, Shout.* From supermarkets. Use on washable colourfast fabrics on grease and fresh stains before washing. **Always** follow instructions.
PUMICE STONE: From chemists.
RUST REMOVER: *Rustins, Jenolite.* From hardware stores. **Always** follow instructions.
SAND: From builders' merchants.
SCOURING PADS: *Goldilocks, Brillo.* From supermarkets. **Always** follow instructions.
SLATE CLEANER: *Bell 1967 Cleaner.* From hardware stores (or see p.33). **Always** follow instructions.
SOAP: *Fairy Snow, Persil* (powder); *Lux Flakes, Boots Soap Flakes, Fairy* (block). From supermarkets. **Always** follow instructions.
STERILISING AGENT: *Milton.* From chemists. **Always** follow instructions.
STONE CLEANER: *Bell 1967 Cleaner, Bell 1966 Cleaner,* for heavy stains. From hardware stores (or see p.33). **Always** follow instructions.
SUEDE CLEANER: *Meltonian* (fabrics); *Miss Dylon* (shoes). From shoe repair stores and department stores. **Always** follow instructions.
TEA AND COFFEE STAIN REMOVER: *Crockclean.* From hardware stores.
TILE BLEACH: From tile merchants. Toxic. **Always** follow instructions.
TILE POLISH: *Cardinal.* From hardware stores. **Always** follow instructions.
TURPENTINE: From hardware stores. Inflammable. **Fabrics: Never** use on acetate, triacetate, modacrylic or viscose (rayon) fabrics. **Always** test first.
UPHOLSTERY SHAMPOO: *1001 Dry-Foam, Bissell Upholstery Shampoo, Sabco Carpet & Upholstery Shampoo.* From hardware and department stores. **Always** follow instructions.
UPHOLSTERY SPOTTING KIT: *Bissell Upholstery Kit.* From department stores. **Always** follow instructions.
VINEGAR: See White/Malt Vinegar.
VINYL UPHOLSTERY CLEANER: *Son-of-a-gun, Turtle Wax Minute Cream.* From motor accessory shops. **Always** follow instructions.
VITREOUS ENAMEL CLEANER: *Jif, Ajax, Flash.* From supermarkets. **Always** follow instructions.
WASHING SODA: *ICI.* From supermarkets. **Always** follow instructions.
WASHING-UP LIQUID: *Fairy, Palmolive, Sqezy, Sunlight.* From supermarkets.
WATER SOFTENER: *Calgon.* From supermarkets. **Always** follow instructions.
WAX POLISH: See Floor/Furniture Polishes.
WEED KILLER: From garden centres. **Always** follow instructions. Poisonous.
WHITE SPIRIT: See Turpentine.
WHITE VINEGAR (DILUTE ACETIC ACID): From supermarkets. **Fabrics: Never** use on acetate or triacetate fabrics. **Always** test first. Use ammonia solution if colour is affected. Use 1 tablespoon/15 ml to 1 pint/500 ml warm water. Use to counteract discolouration from ammonia or other mild alkalies, or use lemon juice.
WHITING: From artists' supply shops. **Always** follow instructions.
WOOD BLEACH: *Rustins Wood Bleach.* From hardware stores. **Always** follow instructions.

Note
When following the instructions in this book, keep to one set of measures (either imperial or metric) as the conversions are not exact.

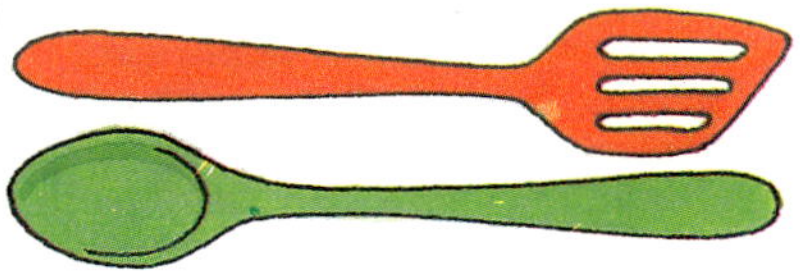

Acrylic utensils

General stains: Wipe immediately with damp cloth.
Stubborn stains: Use all-purpose cleaner. *Or* use moistened bicarbonate of soda.
· **Never** use harsh abrasives.
· **Always** act fast.
See also Plastic Furniture (p. 15).

China

Coffee/tea: Rub with moistened bicarbonate of soda. *Or* use tea and coffee stain remover.
Egg: Wash immediately in cold water. If necessary, rub with moistened salt.
General stains: Use warm mild detergent solution. Rinse.
· **Never** use scouring pads, harsh abrasives, bleach.
· **Always** dry with soft tea towel. Always wash immediately after use.

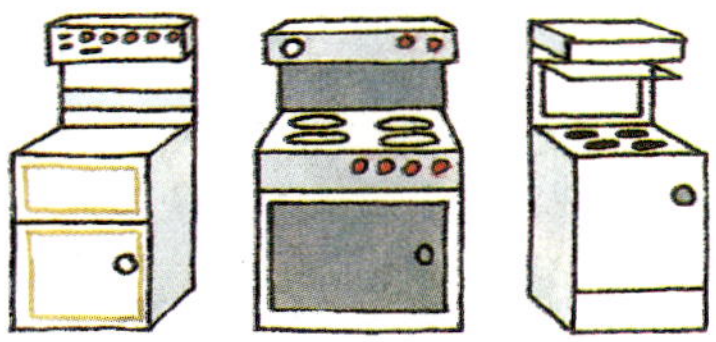

Cookers, gas and electric (exteriors)

General stains: Wipe with warm washing-up liquid solution.
Stubborn stains: Use liquid all-purpose cleaner. Use nylon mesh pad, only if essential. See also Ovens (p. 5), Stainless Steel, (p. 6), and Enamel (p. 8).
Ceramic hobs: Use ceramic hob cleaner.
· **Always** follow manufacturer's instructions. Always wipe up spills and splashes immediately. Always turn electricity off before cleaning. Always check that gas pilot lights are lit after cleaning.

Crockery

Coffee/tea: Rub with vinegar and salt. *Or* rub with moistened bicarbonate of soda. *Or* use tea and coffee stain remover.
Cracked crockery: Boil in a pan of milk for 45 minutes.
Grease: Add a few tablespoons of vinegar to washing-up water.
See also Earthenware.

Crystal/cut glass, including chandeliers

General stains: Rinse in 1:3 vinegar and warm water solution. Dry naturally.
Chandeliers: Use ammonia solution plus washing-up liquid. Wear cotton gloves, dip hands in solution and rub crystal clean.
· **Never** put crystal or cut glass in the dishwasher.

Cutlery

See Knives (p. 5) and Silver, Stainless Steel (p. 9).

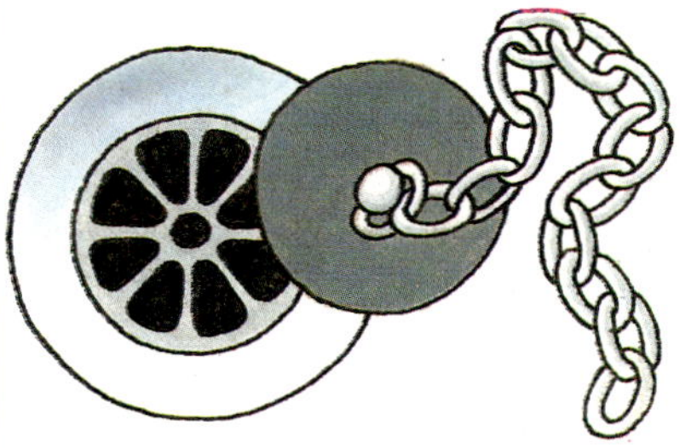

Drains

Grease-blocked: Pour 1 quart/1 litre boiling water plus handful washing soda down outlet. *Or* use cup salt and cup bicarbonate of soda followed by boiling water.
Bad blockage: Use drain cleaner. *Or* call plumber.

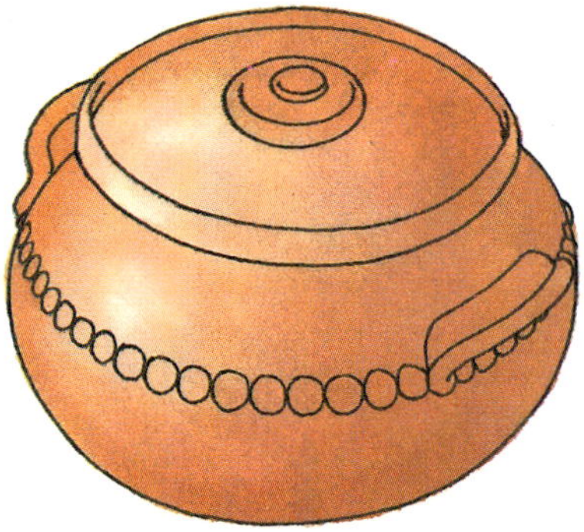

Earthenware

Burnt-on food: Soak until loose. Wash.
· **Never** place in hot water when cold, or vice versa. Never soak for long.
· **Always** follow manufacturer's cleaning instructions if available.

Freezers

See Refrigerators (p. 6).

Gilt and silver ornamented glass

· **Never** use very hot water, or soak for long. Never use ammonia, washing soda or harsh soaps. Never put in dishwasher.
· **Always** use detergent.

Glass, including carafes and decanters

Interior sediment stains: Soak container for two days in distilled water. Wash. If necessary repeat, adding lemon juice or vinegar to distilled water.
Stubborn interior stains: Swill with vinegar and sand or cooking salt.
Grease: Wipe with methylated spirit.
Small scratches: Use glass cleaner. *Or* rub olive oil or toothpaste into scratches.
General stains: Wash in warm washing-up liquid solution. If glass has been discoloured due to bad storage, add 1 tablespoon/15 ml ammonia. Rinse.
· **Always** rinse well.

See also Ovens, Crystal, Heat-Resistant Cooking Glass and Mirrors (p. 5), Windows (p. 6) and Glass Tables (p. 14).

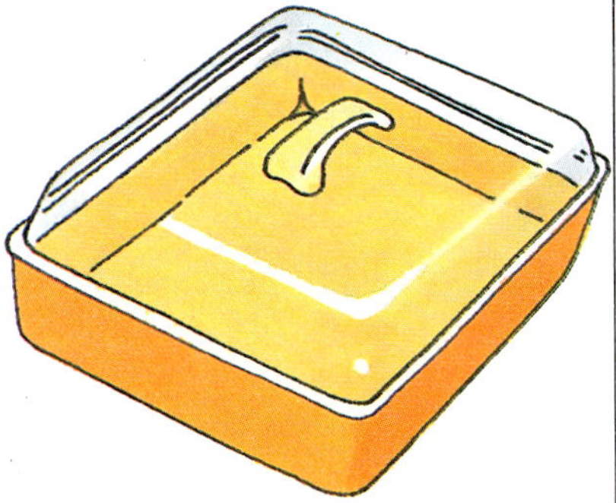

Heat-resistant cooking glass (Pyrex)

Burnt-on food: Soak in warm washing-up solution.
Grease: Soak in mild ammonia solution. Wash.
Sugar/starch: Soak in solution of 3 tablespoons/45 ml bicarbonate of soda to 1 quart/1 litre warm water. Wash.
· **Never** put pans on direct flame or heat.
· **Always** rinse well.

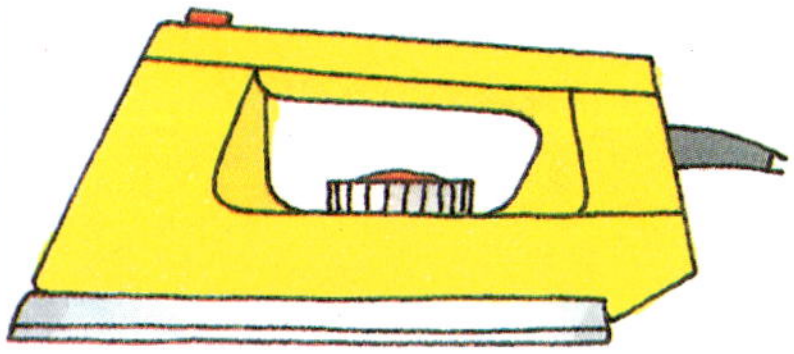

Irons, pressing (non-steam)

Melted nylon: Heat iron and scrape off with a wood spatula.
General stains: *Aluminium soleplate:* Use fine steel wool or abrasive powder. *Or* use iron cleaner.
Non-stick soleplate: Use soapy sponge or nylon mesh pad.
· **Never** use abrasives near chromium plating or on non-stick surfaces.
· **Always** check manufacturer's cleaning instructions.

Irons, pressing (steam)

Burnt-on spots: Rub with hot salt and vinegar solution.
Fur deposits: Use kettle de-scaler or consult professionals (see p. 33).
Wax build-up: **1** Rub with very fine sandpaper. **2** Polish with fine steel wool. **3** Wipe with damp cloth.
General stains: See Non-Steam Irons.
· **Never/Always:** See Non-Steam Irons.

Kettles (exteriors)

See Metals (pp. 8–9).
· **Always** unplug electric kettles before cleaning. Always follow manufacturer's cleaning instructions.

Kettles (interiors)

Fur or scale deposits: Use kettle de-scaler. *Or* boil kettle with 50:50 vinegar and water solution. Leave overnight. Rinse well.
· **Always** follow manufacturer's cleaning instructions.

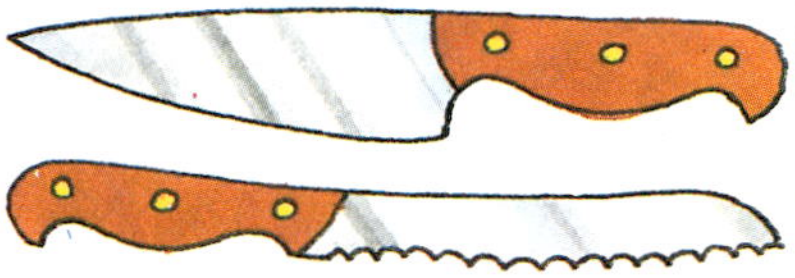

Knives (carbon steel blades)

General stains: Rub with nylon scouring pad.
Stubborn stains: Polish blade with abrasive powder on the end of a cork. *Or* use wet and dry abrasive paper.
· **Never** soak in water or put in the dishwasher.
· **Always** dry thoroughly immediately after washing.
See also Stainless Steel (p. 9).

Knives (horn, bone or ivory handles)

General stains: Use warm soapy water.
· **Never** soak in water.

Melamine tableware

Coffee/tea: Use sterilising agent. *Or* rub with bicarbonate of soda. *Or* fill with hot water plus denture cleaning tablets. Leave one hour. Wash. *Or* use tea and coffee stain remover.
Stubborn stains: Use melamine cleaner.
· **Never** use abrasive cleaners. Never put near direct flame.
· **Always** wash immediately after use.

Mirrors

Hair spray: Use methylated spirit then glass cleaner.
General stains: Wash with mild vinegar or ammonia solution. *Or* use cool tea. *Or* use glass cleaner.
Stubborn stains: Wash with mild borax solution.
· **Never** wet the backing.
· **Always** buff with a soft cloth.

Mother-of-pearl handles

General stains: Use paste of powdered whiting and water. Rub on gently. Wash off with warm soapy water. *Or* use non-abrasive liquid furniture polish.
Stubborn stains: Consult professionals (see p. 33).
· **Never** use ammonia. Never soak in water or put in dishwasher.

Ovens

General stains: Wipe with warm washing-up liquid solution. *Or* use liquid all-purpose cleaner.
Stubborn stains: Use oven cleaner. *Or* **1** Switch off. **2** Place 1 pint/500 ml hot water plus 2 tablespoons/30 ml ammonia in warm oven. Leave overnight. **3** Air. Then wash with warm soapy water.
Glass doors: Rub with bicarbonate of soda. *Or* use washing soda. *Or* use liquid all-purpose cleaner.
· **Never** use abrasives on non-stick surfaces. Never use aerosol oven cleaner on warm glass.
· **Always** follow manufacturer's instructions. Always check that cleaner is suitable for vitreous enamel oven linings.
See also Cookers (p. 4).

Porcelain

See China (p. 4).

Pots and pans

See Metals (pp. 8–9).

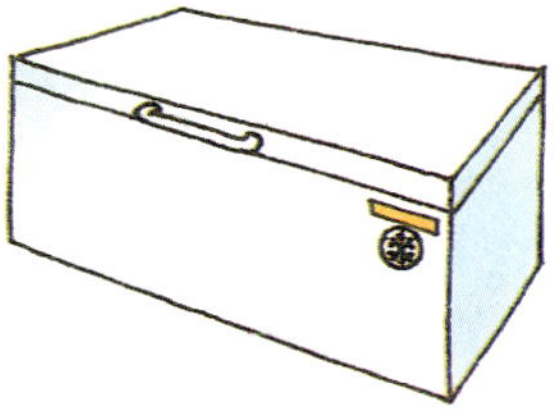

Refrigerators/freezers

General stains: *Exteriors:* Use warm detergent solution. Rub dry.
Interiors: Use moistened bicarbonate of soda.
· **Never** use abrasives.
· **Always** dry well.

Silver cutlery

See Silver (p. 9).

Sinks, stainless steel

Rust: Rub with lighter fuel. Clean as usual.
Water spots: Rub with white vinegar or methylated spirit. Rinse immediately.
General stains: Use washing-up liquid.
· **Never** use harsh abrasives, scouring pads, salt, vinegar, steel wool or undissolved detergent powder.
· **Always** rinse and dry after use.
See also Stainless Steel (p. 9).

Sinks, vitreous enamel

General stains: Use vitreous enamel cleaner.
Blue/green drip stains: Use a vitreous enamel cleaner or soapsuds plus ammonia.
Hard water marks: See Drip Stains, repeat if necessary.
Rust: See Drip Stains. *Or* use a bath stain remover with rust-removing properties. Rub light stains with a cut lemon. Stubborn stains with borax and lemon juice paste.
Stubborn stains: **1** Rub with bleach solution. *Or* apply paste of cream of tartar and dilute hydrogen peroxide. **2** Scrub. **3** If necessary, add 2 drops ammonia to paste. Leave 2 hours. **4** Scrub. Rinse.
· **Never** use harsh abrasives or strong bleaches.
· **Always** rinse well after use. Always clean fixtures according to the material of which they are made.
See also Baths, Vitreous/Porcelain Enamel (p. 7).

Taps

· **Never** use abrasives.
See also Chromium-plating (p. 8), Gold (p. 9).

Teapots

See China (p. 4), Aluminium (p. 8), Silver (p. 9).

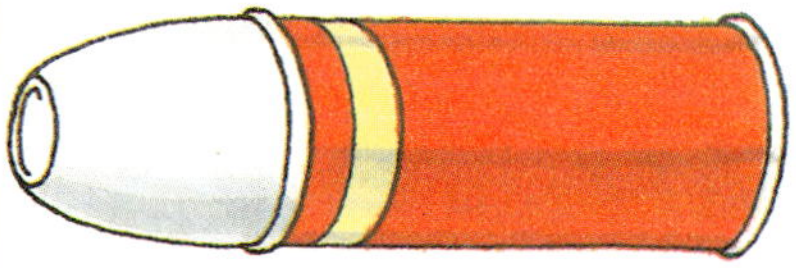

Thermos flasks (interiors)

Coffee/tea: Put crushed eggshell inside with a little hot water. Shake well. Wash. *Or* use tea and coffee stain remover.
General stains: Fill with warm water and 1 tablespoon/15 ml bicarbonate of soda. Leave three hours. Wash.
· **Never** immerse entire bottle in water.
· **Always** rinse well.

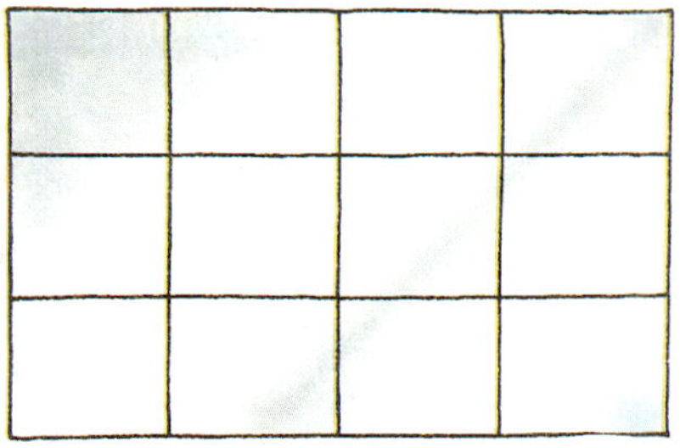

Wall tiles

General stains: *Aluminium:* Wipe with hot washing-up liquid solution.
See also Aluminium (p. 8).
Ceramic: See Ceramic Tiles (p. 10).
Mirrored: See Mirrors (p. 5).

Windows

Paint: If fresh, use turpentine/liquid drycleaner/nail varnish remover. If dried, soften with turpentine. Scrape off.
Putty: Use ammonia. *Or* soften with turpentine. Scrape off.
General stains: See Mirrors (p. 5).
· **Never** scrub dirty glass with dry cloth. Never use soap. Never clean windows when the sun is shining, or in frosty weather.

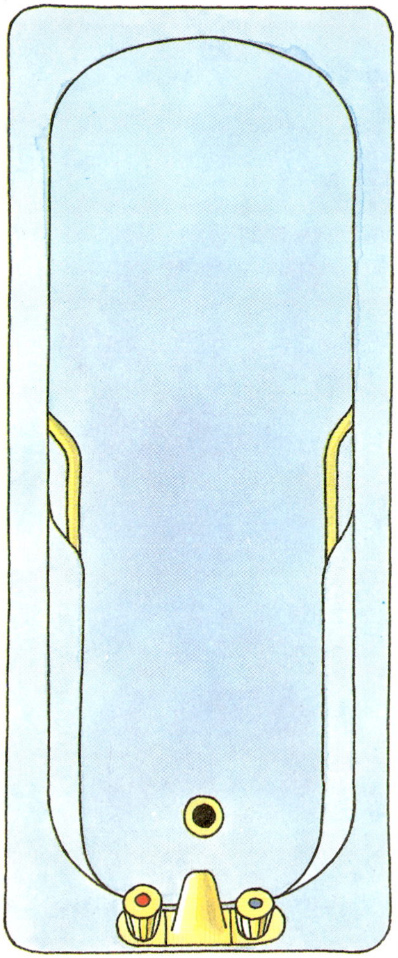

Baths, acrylic/fibreglass

Grease: Use warm washing soda solution.
Light scratches: Rub with silver metal polish.
General stains: Wipe with washing-up liquid or soap.
Stubborn stains: **1** Gently rub with progressively finer wet abrasive paper, until surface is smooth. **2** Rub with silver metal polish.
· **Never** use bath-foam, bath-cubes etc. Never use harsh abrasives or any abrasives.
· **Always** rinse both well after use.

Baths, vitreous/porcelain enamel

General stains: Use bath cleaner or vitreous enamel cleaner.
Yellowed bathtub: Rub with salt and turpentine solution.
Tide marks: **1** See General Stains. *Or* rub with white spirit. **2** Wash off at once with washing-up liquid.
See also Sinks, Vitreous Enamel (p. 6).
· **Never/Always:** See Sinks, Vitreous Enamel (p. 6).

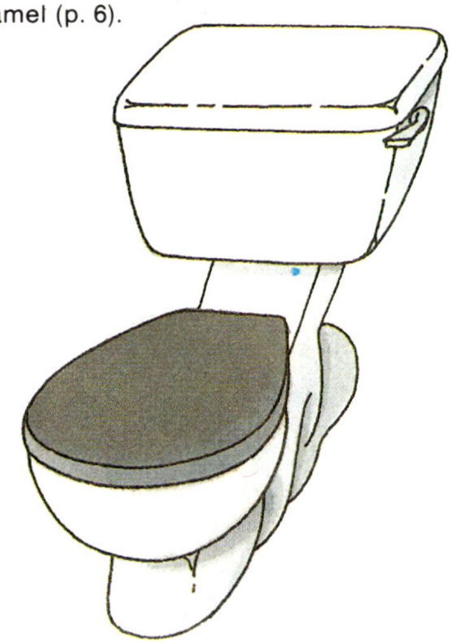

Lavatory

Calcium rings: Gently rub with fine pumice stone or abrasive paper.
General stains: *Bowl:* Apply paste of borax and lemon juice to wet surface. Leave 2 hours. Scrub. *Or* use bleach. *Or* use lavatory cleaner.
Seat: Clean regularly with warm water and disinfectant.
· **Never** mix cleaning agents.

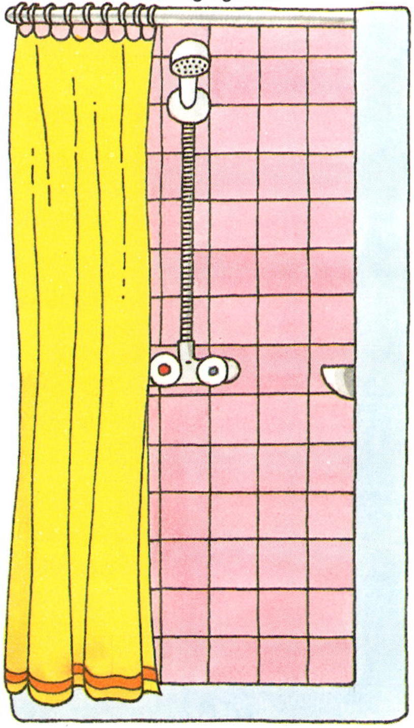

Shower curtains

Mildew: Wipe with weak bleach solution. Wash.
General stains: Sponge with soapsuds or mild detergent. Rinse. Dry naturally.
· **Never** rub, squeeze or wring plastic or rubber shower curtains.
· **Always** test first. Always follow manufacturer's care instructions.

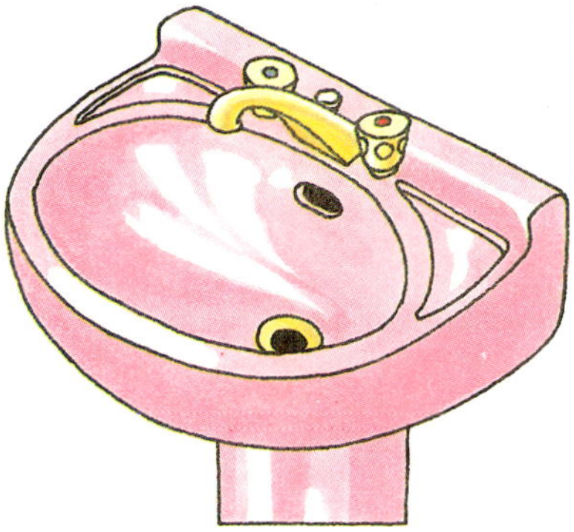

Sinks, fireclay

General stains: Use bath cleaner.
Stubborn stains: Use abrasive powder. *Or* line sink with paper towels and saturate with bleach. Leave for 30 minutes. Remove. Rinse.
See also Sinks, Vitreous Enamel (p. 6).

Wall tiles

Mirrored: See Mirrors (p. 5).
See also Wall Tiles (p. 6).

Metals

Metals, general

· **Never** use harsh abrasives.
· **Always** identify metal before cleaning. If in doubt use a metal polish for soft metals.

Aluminium (pots and pans)

Burnt-on food: Fill pan with water. Boil. Scrape with wooden spoon. Wash.
General stains: Soak in solution 1 tablespoon/15 ml borax to 1 pint/500 ml hot water. Wash as usual.
Stubborn stains: Simmer strong solution of cream of tartar or vinegar for 20 minutes. Wash.
Teapots: **General stains:** Fill with water and 2 teaspoons/10 ml borax. Leave 2 hours. Wash.
· **Never** put coloured aluminium in dishwasher. Never treat non-stick or mirror-finishes with abrasive cleaners or sharp implements. Never use washing soda. Never store food in aluminium.
· **Always** clean with soap-filled pad rubbing in one direction only. Always rinse thoroughly.
See also Metal Furniture (p. 14), Wall Tiles (p. 6).

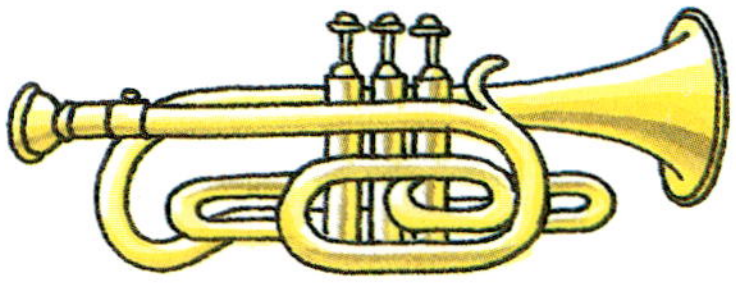

Brass

Corrosion: Boil small objects in water containing salt and vinegar. Then use brass metal polish.
Tarnished: See Copperware.
General stains: Use neat brass metal polish or mix it with lemon juice. *Or* see Copperware.
Stubborn stains: Clean with strong ammonia solution. Polish.
Brass fire tools: Rub with fine steel wool in one direction only. Polish.
· **Always** consult professionals on antique pieces (see p. 33).

Bronze

Green spots/verdigris: Rub with brown leather polish. Buff. *Or* brush with stiff brush. Then swab with 10% acetic acid solution. Rinse, dry, buff and polish.
General stains: *Lacquered bronze:* If cracked or peeling, re-lacquer.
Unlacquered bronze: Wash with mild soap or detergent solution. *Or* wash with hot vinegar or buttermilk. Rinse. Polish.
Stubborn stains: Wash in hot soapy water or rub with pure turpentine/paraffin. When dry, brush with stiff brush. Polish.
· **Never** use wire brush or harsh abrasives.
· **Always** consult professionals on antique pieces (see p. 33).

Cast iron, pots and pans (uncoated)

Burnt-on food: Fill pan with water and a little washing soda. Boil. Wash.
Rust: Use steel wool and abrasive cleaner.
Stubborn stains: Use steel wool or scouring pad.
· **Never** use synthetic detergents. Never store pans with lids on.
· **Always** rinse and dry well. Always coat thinly with oil before storing.

Cast iron, pots and pans (coated)

If coated with enamel, see Enamelware, if non-stick, see Non-Stick Pots and Pans (p. 9).

Chromium-plating

Grease: Apply moistened bicarbonate of soda. *Or* use whiting or chrome metal polish.
Green spots/corrosion: Use chrome metal polish for mild corrosion. Replace or re-plate badly corroded taps, pipes etc.
General stains: Wash with warm, soapy water. Dry. *Or* use ammonia or chrome metal polish.
· **Never** use abrasives.
· **Always** use cleaning agents sparingly.

Copperware

Green stains: Use soapsuds plus a few drops of ammonia.
Tarnished: Rub with a cut lemon dipped in salt. *Or* use copper metal polish.
General stains: Rub with paste of vinegar, salt and flour. Wash.
· **Always** wash thoroughly after using acids or proprietary polishes.

Enamelware

Burnt-on food: Fill pan with cold water plus 2 teaspoons/10 ml bicarbonate of soda. Boil. Wash as usual.
Grease stains: Use all-purpose cleaner.
General stains: Rub with moistened bicarbonate of soda. *Or* soak in hot detergent solution. *Or* use an all-purpose cleaner.
Stubborn stains: Fill pan with cold water plus 1 teaspoon/5 ml bleach. Leave 3 hours. Wash.
· **Never** use harsh abrasives. Never use to store acid foods.

Gold

Tarnished: Consult professionals (see p. 33).
General stains: Use soft metal polish. Buff.
· **Never** clean plated items too often.

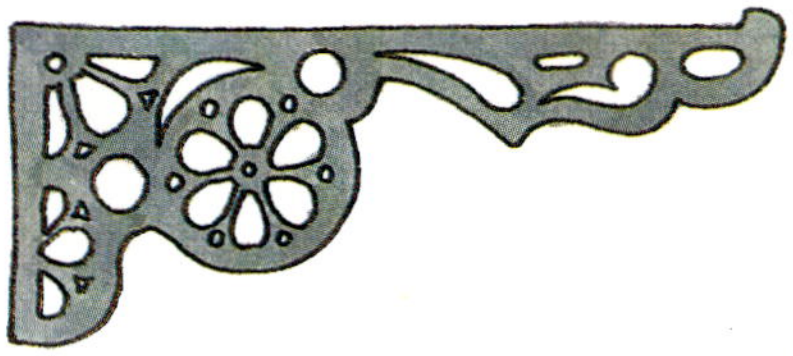

Iron

Rust: Rub with paraffin-moistened steel wool.
Rusty hinges: Lubricate with penetrating oil.
Stubborn rust stains: If possible, soak in paraffin. Then rub with steel wool. *Or* use rust remover.
See also Irons, Pressing/Steam (p. 5).

Jewellery

· **Always** treat carefully. Consult jewellery repairers if necessary.
See also Metals.

Lead

White deposits: **1** If possible, boil in several changes of water. **2** Place in 1 part vinegar to 9 parts water. **3** Rinse in water plus 1 teaspoon/5 ml bicarbonate of soda. **4** Rinse in distilled water.
General stains: Scrub with turpentine.
Stubborn stains: Use abrasive powder.

Nickel

General stains: Use whiting/fine abrasive powder moistened with methylated spirit. Wash. Rinse, buff. *Or* use metal polish.
· **Always** clean frequently.

Non-stick pots and pans

General stains: Follow manufacturer's instructions.
Stubborn stains: Boil solution of 1 cup/225 ml water, 2 tablespoons/30 ml bicarbonate of soda, $\frac{1}{2}$ cup/100 ml bleach in pan for 5–10 minutes. Wash.
· **Never** use abrasives.
· **Always** dry well and lightly oil before storing.

Pewter/Britannia metal

Grease: Rub with methylated spirit. Wash.
General stains: Wash with soapy water. Dry. *Or* rub with cabbage leaf.
Stubborn stains: Rub with fine steel wool and olive oil. *Or* rub with paste of mild abrasive powder and olive oil. *Or* consult professionals (see p. 33).

Silver and silverplate, including cutlery

Egg tarnish: Rub with table salt.
Food stains: Wash immediately after use. Dry.
General stains: Hand rub with paste of French chalk (absorbent powder), ammonia and methylated spirit. *Or* use silver metal polish. *Or* use moistened cigarette ash. Wash, rinse and dry.
Teapots: Place 1 tablespoon/15 ml washing soda plus several foil milk bottle tops in teapot. Fill with boiling water. Leave 1 hour. Rinse.
· **Never** bring silver into contact with rubber. Never use abrasives or bleach. Never wrap in newspaper. Never clean on stainless steel sink.
· **Always** wash before and after polishing. Always dry thoroughly immediately after washing. Always store carefully.
See also Candle Holders (p. 16).

Stainless steel, including cutlery, pots and pans

Rings around the edge: Use methylated spirit. Wash thoroughly.
Burnt-on food: Use mild abrasive cleaner or scouring pad.
Pitting: Use fine steel wool. Polish.
General stains: Wash with hot soapy water. *Or* use stainless steel metal polish.
Teapots: Fill with boiling water plus 1 tablespoon/15 ml washing soda. Leave 1 hour. Rinse.
· **Never** use harsh abrasives, bleach, salt or silver dip. Never get near direct flame, or soak in vinegar or other food acids.
· **Always** wash promptly after use. Always rinse well. Always avoid hot grease/fat splashes.
See also Knives (p. 5) and Sinks (p. 6).

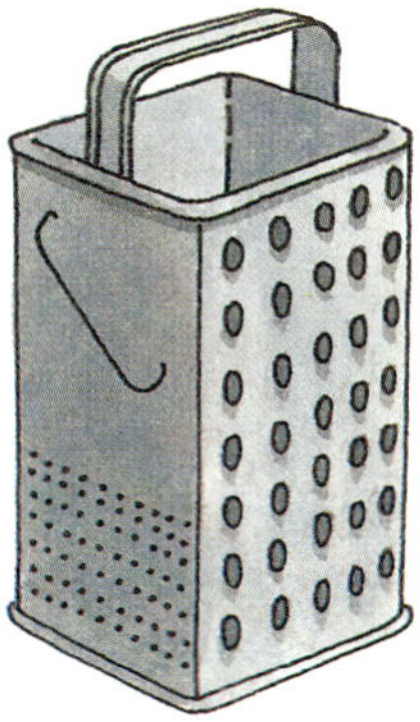

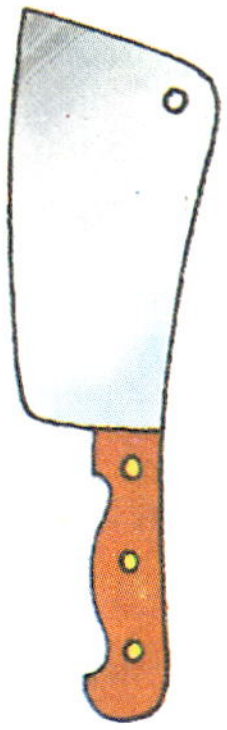

Steel

Burnt-on food: Fill pan with washing-up liquid solution. Boil. Wash as usual.
Rust stains: Use rust remover.
General stains: Use abrasive powder/fine steel wool/medium emery cloth. Wash. Dry.
· **Never** bring into contact with acids or water for long periods of time. Never put hot pans into washing-up water without cooling first.
· **Always** protect your eyes when cleaning steel. Always dry steel pots and pans well and lightly oil before storing.

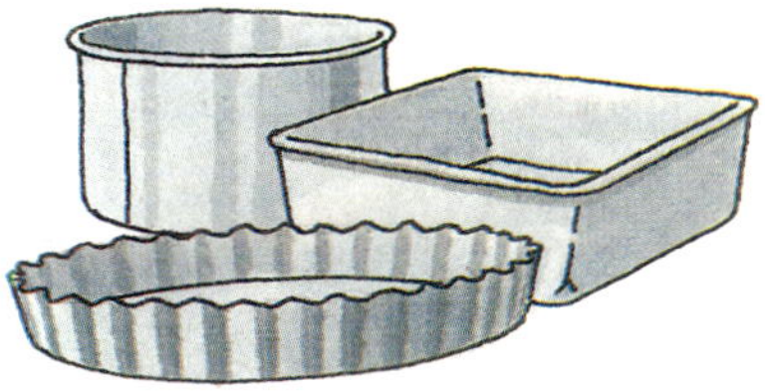

Tinned ware

Grease: Wash in hot washing soda solution. Rinse.
Rust: Rub with potato dipped in mild abrasive powder. Wash.
General stains: Wash immediately after use in hot washing-up liquid solution. Rinse.
Stubborn stains: Boil item in strong washing soda solution. Wash.
· **Never** use harsh abrasives.
· **Always** dry thoroughly.
See also Knives, Carbon Steel (p. 4) and Metal Furniture (p. 14).

Zinc

Tarnish: Rub with vinegar or lemon juice solution. Leave 5 minutes. Rinse, dry and polish.
General stains: Use hot soapy water.
Stubborn stains: Use mild abrasive powder.

Alabaster

Nicotine stains: Wipe with turpentine. Buff.
General stains: Use washing-up liquid solution.
Stubborn stains: Consult professionals (see p. 33).
· **Never** immerse in water.

Asphalt, bitumastic, mastic, pitchmastic, semastic, thermoplastic

General stains: Rub lightly with wire wool. Rinse. Polish.
· **Never** use wax polish.

Brickwork (calcium silicate and clay)

Lichens and mosses: Use weed killer. Growth indicates damp. Treat.
Tar: **1** Remove excess, unless liable to damage bricks. **2** Scrub with detergent solution.

See also Brick Walls (p. 12).

· **Never** use soap. Never apply chemicals directly.
· **Always** test first. Leave 1 week before proceeding. Always consult professionals (see p. 33) for large areas of cleaning and before cleaning calcium silicate brickwork, especially if using acids. Always saturate with clean water before and after using chemicals. Always wear protective clothing and ensure good ventilation.

Cement, concrete and stone

Coffee/tea: Scrub with hot soapy water. *Or* apply bleach solution. Rinse.
Ink: Apply bleach solution.
Oil/grease: Scrub with heavy detergent solution or slate cleaner. Rinse. *Or* sprinkle with an absorbent powder. After a while, sweep up.
Paint (emulsion): Rub with acetone.
Paint (oil): Use paint remover. Follow manufacturer's instructions.
Rust: Use rust remover or concrete cleaner. Follow manufacturer's instructions.
Timber (yellow/brown): Scrub vigorously with bleach solution. Rinse.
General stains: Scrub with detergent or washing soda solution.
Stubborn stains: Repeat as above. *Or* scrub with strong bleach solution.
· **Never** use soap or scouring powder. Never use acid on limestone.
· **Always** scrape off or mop up deposit before applying chemicals. Always rinse with clear water after treatment.

Ceramic (glazed) tiles

Cloudy film on surface: Use water softener.
Iron: Use abrasive powder.
Lime: Apply neat vinegar. Leave 10 minutes. Wash.
Paint: **1** Wipe immediately and scour. **2** If necessary, use commercial tile bleach or paint remover. Test first. Follow instructions. *Or* place a thick cloth saturated with hydrogen peroxide over stain. Cover first cloth with cloth moistened with ammonia. Repeat if necessary.
Soap scum: Use paraffin.
Stains between tiles: Brush with bleach solution. *Or* re-grout.
General stains: Use mild detergent solution. *Or* wash with solution $\frac{1}{2}$ cup/100 ml ammonia, $\frac{1}{2}$ cup/100 ml vinegar, $\frac{1}{4}$ cup/50 ml washing soda and 1 gallon/4 litres warm water.
Stubborn stains: 1. See General Stains. *Or* scrub with paste of bicarbonate of soda and bleach. *Or* consult professional tile cleaner.
· **Never** apply a damp cloth to tiles whilst hot or if near a fire. Never use acid solution or harsh abrasives on tiles.
· **Always** rinse thoroughly.

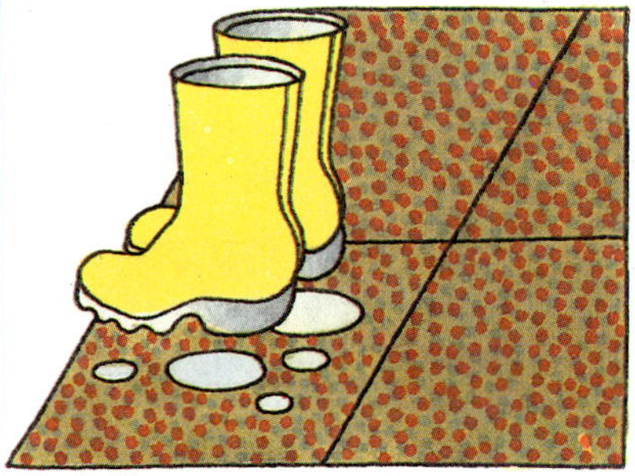

Cork tiles

See Plastic Films/Seals and Cork Walls (p. 12).

Enamel

See Enamelware (p. 8).

Laminated plastic (Arborite, Formica, melamine-faced chipboard, PVC, Warerite)

Cochineal, coffee, fruit juices, hair-dye,

iodine, nail-varnish remover, tea, wine (red): Mop up immediately with hot soapy water.
Food and ink: Rub in neat washing-up liquid or liquid all-purpose cleaner.
Stubborn stains: Wash with hot soapy water. *Or* apply paste of bicarbonate of soda and water. Rub off after 2 minutes.
· **Never** use abrasives.
· **Always** mop stains up quickly.

Leather desktops

See Leather (p. 17).

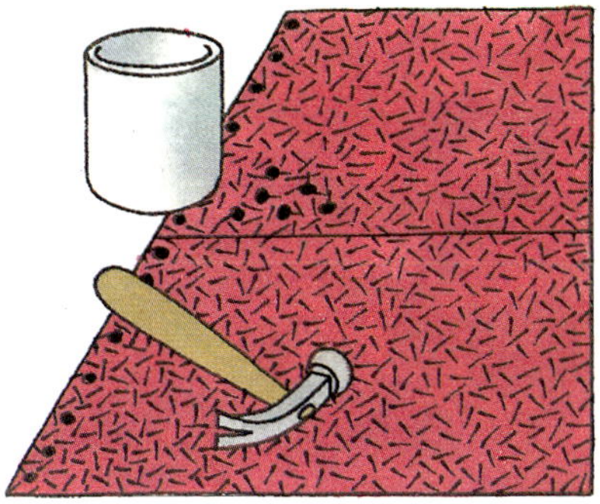

Linoleum

Crayon: Rub with silver metal polish.
Scuff marks: Rub with emulsion floor polish.
General stains: Use all purpose cleaner or washing soda solution.
· **Never** use harsh soaps or scouring powders. Never leave oil or water standing on linoleum. Dry well after washing.

Marble

Cosmetics, foliage, non-metallic ink, tea, tobacco: Apply hydrogen peroxide solution plus a few drops of ammonia. Leave 2 hours. Rinse. Dry.
Grease/oil: Rub with alcohol/acetone/lighter fuel. Rinse. Dry.
Rust: Use rust remover. Rinse. Dry.
Wine, coffee, alcohol, spirits, cigarette burns: Consult professionals.
General stains: Use liquid abrasive cleaner/lemon juice/vinegar. Rinse, dry.
Stubborn stains: As above. *Or* apply a paste of marble cleaner and water. Rinse off when dry.
· **Never** use heavy detergents, acids, petrol, paraffin or white spirit.
· **Always** wipe up spills immediately with warm soapy water. Always rinse well and buff with soft cloth. Always consult professional marble cleaner (see p. 33) for antique marble or if very stained.

Onyx

General stains: Use washing-up liquid solution.
Stubborn stains: Wipe with methylated spirit. *Or* consult professionals (see p. 33).
· **Never** immerse in water.
· **Always** wipe up spills immediately. Always handle as little as possible.

Plastic films/seals

Dull-looking: Rub in toothpaste. Buff.
Water marks: Rub with liquid floor wax polish.
General stains: Clean with liquid abrasive cleaner or detergent.
· **Never** cut on surface. Never use abrasives or wire wool. Never put extreme heat on surface.
· **Always** wipe up spills immediately.

Quarry tiles

White patches: Wash with 1 tablespoon/15 ml vinegar to 1 pint/500 ml water solution. Do not rinse. Repeat if necessary.
General stains: Mop with liquid abrasive cleaner solution.

Rubber

Scuff marks: Rub with abrasive cleaner. Rinse.
General stains: Wash with soapy water. Rinse.
· **Never** put anything hot on rubber. Never use detergent, petrol, paraffin, wax-polish, or white spirit. Never wash unless necessary.
· **Always** remove fat, grease, oil, petrol, spirits and fruit juices immediately.

Slate

Grease: Use oil stain remover.
General stains: Use washing soda solution. Rinse.
Stubborn stains: Repeat as above. *Or* use slate cleaner.
· **Always** rinse well.

Vinyl/vinyl asbestos

Scuff marks: Use soft pencil rubber. *Or* use emulsion floor polish.
General stains: Use warm soapy water and rub gently with wire wool. If necessary, add all-purpose cleaner.
· **Never** use petrol, paraffin, lighter fuel, white spirit or wax polish.
· **Always** check manufacturer's care instructions. Always rinse well.
See also Upholstery, Vinyl (p. 27) and Wallcoverings, Vinyl (p. 13).

Wooden floors/work surfaces

General stains: *Untreated wood:* Use detergent and as little water as possible. *Or* scrub with scouring powder.
Painted wood: Wash with washing-up liquid solution. *Or* use hot water plus 1 teaspoon/5 ml washing soda per gallon/4 litres. Rinse.
Sealed/varnished wood: Rub with cold tea. *Or* use liquid abrasive cleaner.
Waxed wood: Use mild detergent solution. *Or* fine steel wool dipped in liquid floor/furniture wax. Polish.
White spots and rings: Rub with wood ash and raw potato or salad oil. *Or* rub with moistened cigarette ash or mayonnaise.
· **Never** over-wet. Never use abrasives.
· **Always** wipe up spills immediately.
See also Wooden Furniture (p. 15) and Wood, Painted (p. 13).

Brick walls (calcium silicate and clay)

Efflorescence (white crystals/furry deposit): Wash repeatedly with water. Let bricks dry between washings. *Or* brush wall. Not sandfaced bricks. Never let salts accumulate at foot of wall.

Lime and mortar: If possible, scrape away. Wash.

Oil: Sponge with white spirit.

Paint (graffiti): 1 Use paint remover. When soft, scrape off. **2** Wash with soapy water. **3** If necessary, grind off face of calcium silicate brickwork.

Smoke and soot: Rub with art gum eraser. *Or* scrub with detergent.

See also Brickwork (p. 10).

· **Never/Always:** See Brickwork (p. 10).

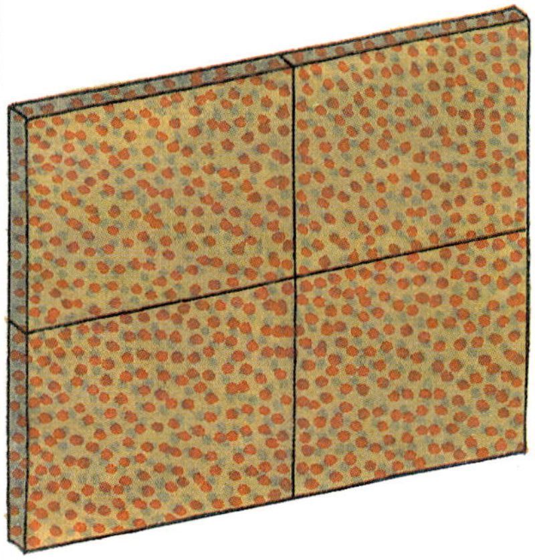

Cork walls

General stains: Sponge gently with warm, mild detergent solution.

· **Never** over-wet.

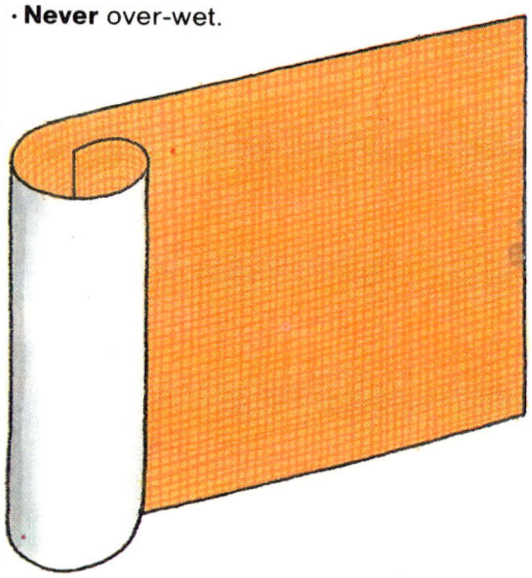

Fabric wallcoverings

General stains: Dab with baby powder. Leave 2 hours. Brush off gently.

· **Never** use dry-cleaner or upholstery cleaners.

· **Always** follow manufacturer's care instructions.

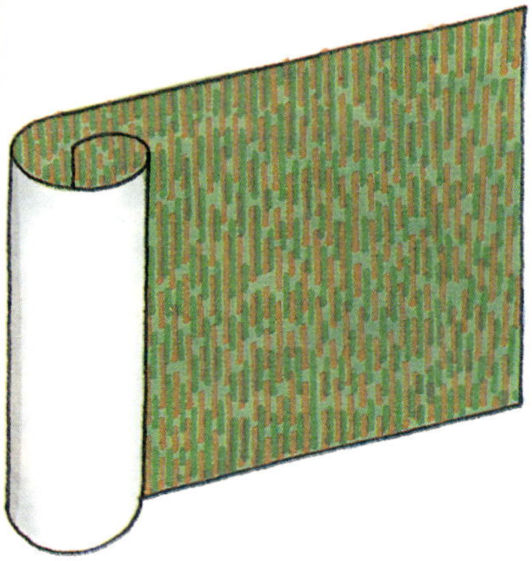

Grasscloth

Grease: Use aerosol dry-cleaner. Follow instructions.

General stains: Dab with baby powder. Leave 2 hours. Brush off gently.

· **Never** use water.

· **Always** test first.

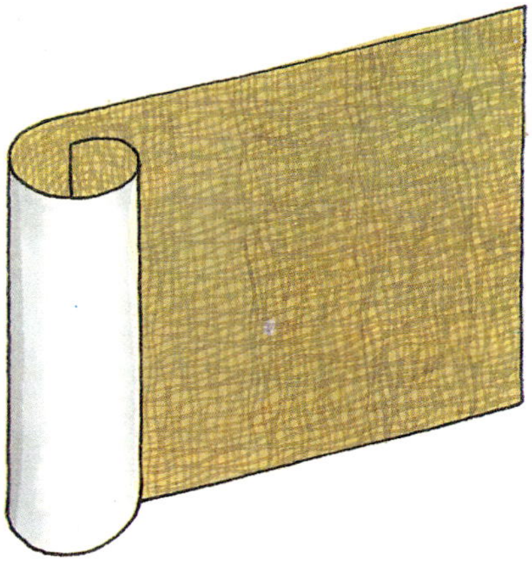

Hessian

Grease: See Grasscloth.

General stains: Dab with baby powder. Leave 2 hours. Brush off gently. *Or* rub with stale white bread.

· **Never** use water.

· **Always** test first.

Painted walls and ceilings (water-based paint)

General stains: Dust. Wash with mild solution of washing-up liquid. Work from bottom up. Clean small areas at a time. Rinse and dry before cleaning next bit.

Stubborn stains: Use mild detergent solution as above.

· **Never** use washing or scouring powders.

· **Always** use clean water and rinse thoroughly. Always turn electricity off at mains.

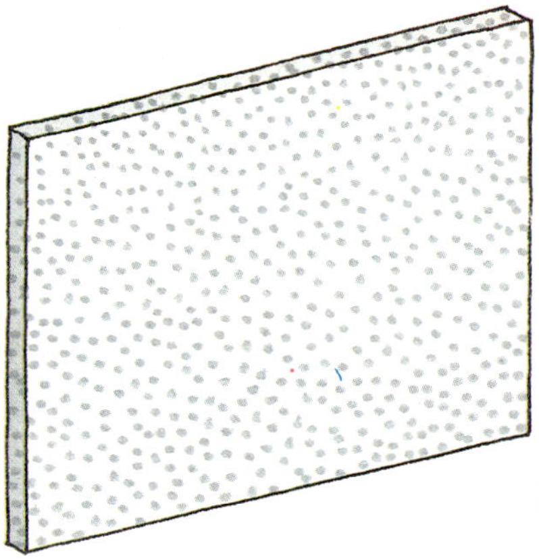

Polystyrene (expanded)

General stains: Sponge with warm mild detergent solution. Rinse.

· **Never** use anything stronger than above. Never apply pressure.

· **Always** leave to dry thoroughly.

Vinyl wallcoverings

Ballpoint ink: Wash immediately with warm soap or detergent solution.

Candle wax: 1 Lift off carefully when hard. **2** Dab remaining colour gently with methylated spirit. **3** If necessary, finish with all-

purpose cleaner.
Crayon: Wipe with damp cloth, then all-purpose cleaner or silver metal polish.
Felt-tip pen: Use all-purpose cleaner/neat washing-up liquid/methylated spirit.
Hair oil: Rub lightly with all-purpose cleaner/white spirit.
General stains: See Painted Walls.
· **Never** over-wet. Never use ammonia, acetone, abrasives or nail-polish remover.
· **Always** work from the bottom up.
See also Vinyl Flooring (p. 11) and Upholstery, Vinyl (p. 27).

Wall-hangings (silk)

· **Always** consult specialist dry cleaner (see p. 33).
See also Silk (p. 18).

Wallpaper, washable

· **Never** over-wet.
· **Always** test first.
See also Painted Walls.

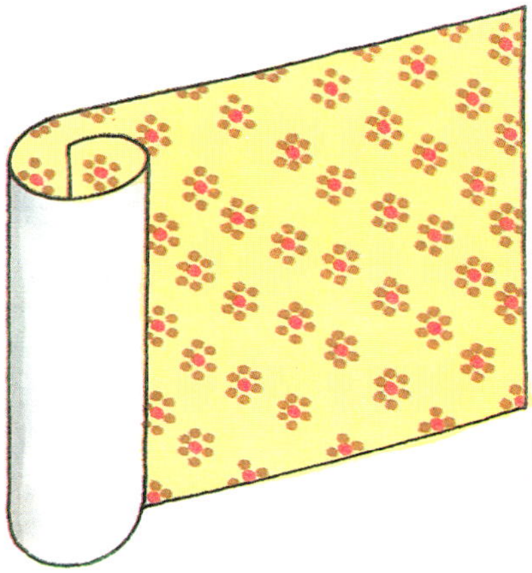

Wallpaper, non-washable

Candle wax: Draw out grease with warm iron on blotting paper over stain, then use dry-cleaner. Occasionally traces left.
Crayon: 1 Sponge lightly with liquid dry-cleaner. **2** Remove residue as for Candle Wax (above). *Or* rub gently with moistened bicarbonate of soda.
Food/grease stains: 1 Draw out grease with warm iron on blotting paper over stain. *Or* apply paste of absorbent powder and dry-cleaning fluid. Brush off when dry. **2** If necessary, rub stain with moistened borax.
Ink: Blot immediately. Do not smear. Then use ink eradicator. Test first.
Lipstick: Use dry-cleaner. Occasionally traces left.
Pencil marks/light smudges: Use an india rubber.
Sellotape (adhesive tape): Remove. Draw out mark with warm iron on blotting paper over stain.
General stains: Rub over with stale white bread.
· **Never** use water.
· **Always** test first.

Wallpaper, textured and embossed

Grease: Dab with baby powder. Leave 2 hours. Brush off gently.
General stains: Sponge with mild detergent solution.
· **Never** press hard. Never over-wet.
· **Always** test first.

Whitewashed walls

· **Always** repaint when stained.

Wood, painted (oil-based paint)

Grease: Use mild detergent solution or all-purpose cleaner.
General stains: Use a paintwork cleaner. *Or* wash with hot, mild washing soda solution. *Or* use washing-up liquid solution.
· **Never** use abrasives.
· **Always** work from the bottom up.

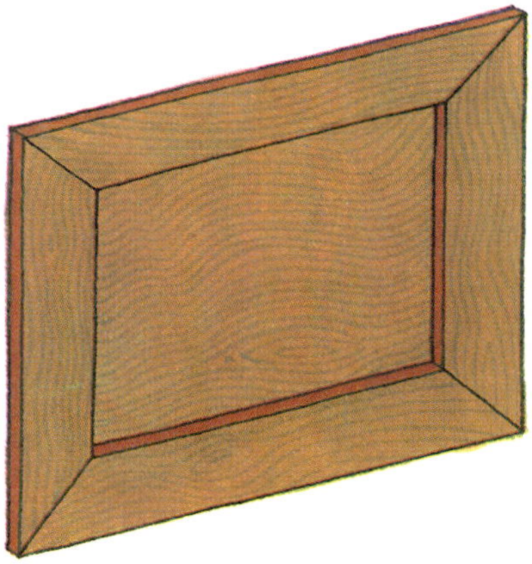

Wood, panelling

Fine scratches: Rub with fine steel wool and white spirit. Rub in the direction of the grain. Polish. Buff.
General stains: *Sealed:* Wash with mild detergent solution. Rinse. Buff.
Wax-finished: Use furniture cleaner.

Furniture, general

· **Always** follow manufacturer's care instructions with modern furniture. Always consult professional restorers with antique furniture. Always identify surfaces before cleaning.

Antique wood

Grease: **1** Rub with chamois leather and solution (1:8) vinegar and water. Dry. Buff. **2** Polish as usual.

General stains: Consult professionals.

· **Never** use modern furniture polishes with added silicones.

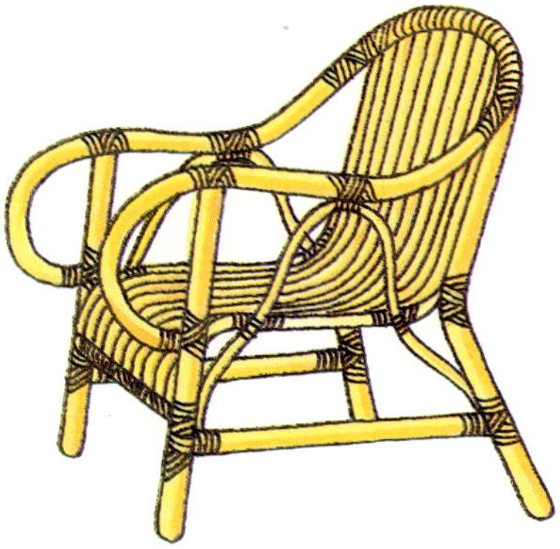

Bamboo furniture

General stains: Scrub gently with warm soapy water plus a little borax. Rinse with salt water.

· **Never** use detergent.

Basketware and cane furniture

General stains: *Varnished furniture:* Wipe with damp cloth. *Or* use mild soapsuds plus a little ammonia. Rinse. Dry.

Unvarnished furniture: **1** Scrub lightly with warm salt water *or* rub with fine steel wool and mild washing soda solution. **2** Rinse with cold water. Dry.

· **Never** over-wet cane.

· **Always** rinse well with cold water.

French polished wood

Alcohol: Wipe up immediately.

Heat/water marks: Rub with solution $\frac{1}{4}$ pint/150 ml turpentine and 1 pint/500 ml linseed oil. Leave 8 hours. Remove and polish. *Or* see White Rings below.

Scratches: Rub with furniture renovator in direction of grain. *Or* use D.I.Y. French polish and follow instructions carefully.

White heat marks: May need to be stripped down surface and re-polished. Consult professional French polisher.

White rings: Saturate cotton wool pad with methylated spirit. Place inside soft white cloth. Carefully rub quickly over surface.

General stains: Rub with solution (1:8) white vinegar and water. Dry well and polish.

Stubborn stains: Consult professionals.

· **Never** place hot or wet things directly onto surface.

· **Always** consult professional French polisher, especially if antique furniture.

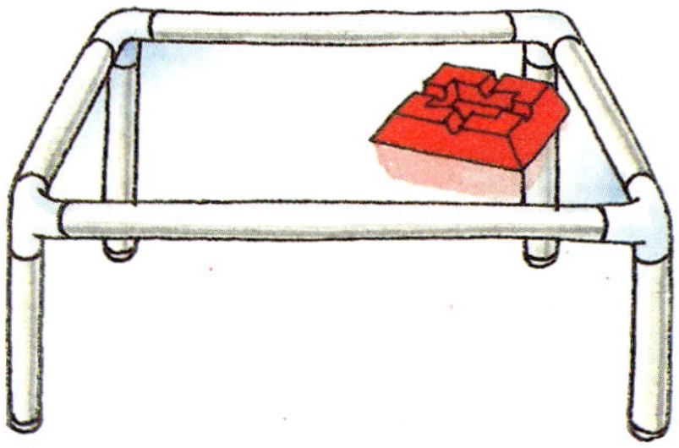

Glass table tops

General stains: **1** Rub with lemon juice or alcohol. **2** Dry with paper towel. **3** Buff with newspaper. *Or* use glass/window cleaner. See also Glass (p. 4), Windows (p. 6).

Lampshades

General stains: *Buckram:* Rub with turpentine.

Fibreglass: Wipe with damp cloth.

Hand-painted silk, linen and chintz: Consult specialist cleaner (see p. 33).

Imitation parchment: Use paste furniture polish. *Or* rub with india rubber.

Metallic paper: Rub with 1 tablespoon/15 ml turpentine plus $\frac{1}{4}$ pint/150 ml paraffin. Wipe off.

Nylon, rayon and silk (detachable shades): **1** Repeatedly dip shade in warm soap/detergent solution. Test first. **2** Rinse in warm water. **3** Dry quickly.

Nylon, rayon and silk (shade glued to frame): Consult specialist cleaner (see p. 33).

Parchment (vellum): Wipe with solution of 1 tablespoon/15 ml soapflakes, 1 tablespoon/15 ml water, 2 tablespoons/30 ml methylated spirit.

Plastic: Wipe with warm, soapy water. Rinse. Pat dry.

· **Always** dust shades regularly. Always clean according to surface. Always switch off the light and unplug before cleaning the shade.

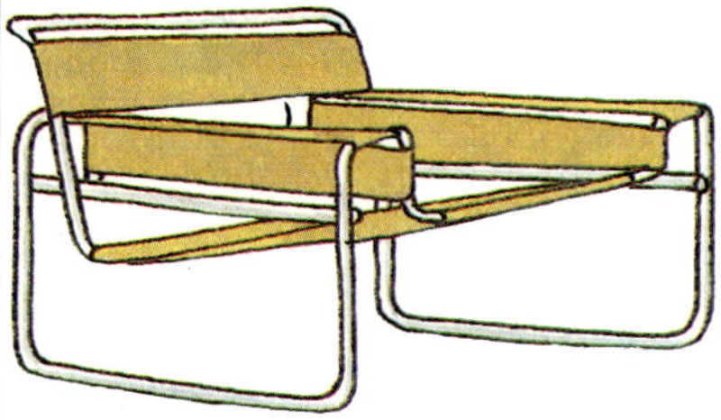

Metal furniture

Aluminium: Use washing-up liquid solution. *Or* rub with fine steel wool in one direction only. *Or* use metal polish.

Grease: Add 1 tablespoon/15 ml borax to washing-up liquid solution.

Tubular steel: Use metal polish.

Rust: Rub with turpentine.

See also Metals (p. 8).

Painted furniture

See Wood, Painted (p. 13).

Plastic furniture (acrylic/perspex and polyurethane)

Scratches: **1** Rub acrylics with soft metal polish. **2** Wipe over with moist cloth. Buff.
General stains: *Acrylics:* Rub with liquid abrasive cleaner. *Or* perspex cleaner.
Polyurethane: Rub with washing-up liquid.
· **Never** use heavy abrasive cleaners, chemicals, acids, petroleum, undiluted bleach or disinfectant, dry-cleaners or acetone.
· **Always** avoid heat.

Wooden furniture

Alcohol: Act fast. **1** Mop up. Rub with palm of hand. **2** Then mop with a little teak oil furniture polish or linseed oil. **3** If necessary, rub with paste of oil plus cigarette ash or powdered pumice. **4** Remove and re-wax.
Blood: **1** Wipe up. **2** Sandpaper surface lightly. **3** Swab on hydrogen peroxide.
Cigarette burns: **1** Treat as Heat Marks. **2** If necessary, lightly sandpaper area. **3** Rebuild with plastic wood or coloured beeswax.
Dents: **1** Fill hole with hot water. *Or* cover with damp cotton cloth and heat with tip of warm iron. Remove when steaming. **2** When dry, re-wax/polish.
Glue: Rub with cold cream/peanut butter/salad oil.
Grease, fats and oil: Rub with lighter fuel. *Veneered or inlaid wood:* Cover thickly with talcum powder. On top place few layers of paper tissues. Heat paper with non-steam iron.
Heat marks (white): **1** Remove finish with methylated spirit. **2** When dry re-colour wood (see Scratches). **3** Re-polish surface.
Cellulose and lacquered finishes: **1** Rub with brass metal polish. **2** Remove before dry. **3** Rub with scorching hot duster. **4** Re-polish.

Oiled wood: Remove finish with methylated spirit. When dry, if necessary, rub in teak oil furniture polish.
Ink: Wash immediately with water. Then dab with lemon juice.
Paint (oil and water based): Old stains: **1** Cover with linseed oil. Leave 1 hour, scrape off carefully. **2** If necessary, apply paste of oil and powdered pumice. **3** Rub off, wipe with oil. **4** Polish.
Paint (oil based): Fresh stains: Wipe with liquid furniture polish or turpentine. Polish.
Paint (water based): Fresh stains: Wipe with soap solution.
Paper: To remove, cover with salad oil. Leave 2 hours. Wipe off.
Red ink stains: **1** See Ink. **2** If necessary, sandpaper wood lightly, place cotton wool saturated with weak solution of oxalic acid on stain. Leave 2 minutes. Wipe off with damp cloth. **3** Re-polish.
Scratches: Rub wax crayons/shoe polish/eyebrow pencil into scratch with cotton wool swab to disguise.

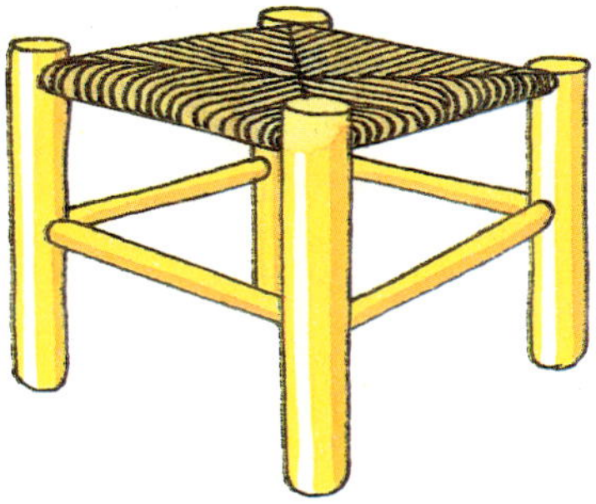

Ebony: Use black (any of the above).
Mahogany: Use dark brown (any of the above).
Maple: Use iodine plus alcohol. Dry. Re-wax.
Red mahogany: Apply iodine with fine brush.
Teak: Sandpaper gently. Then rub with solution (50:50) linseed oil and turpentine.
Walnut: Rub with meat of fresh walnut.
Water marks (white): **1** Rub with very fine steel wool and oil in the direction of the grain. *Or* apply a paste of mayonnaise or olive oil and cigarette ash. **2** Buff with damp cloth. *Or* **1** Apply solution (50:50) linseed oil and turpentine. Leave for 2 hours. **2** Remove with vinegar.

Water marks (black): Brush on saturated solution of oxalic acid. Leave 2–3 seconds. Remove with damp cloth. *Or* rub surface gently with fine steel wool until fresh wood is reached. Re-colour or stain wood. See Scratches. Re-polish or oil.
· **Never** use too much water on wood. Never use oiled or treated dusters on furniture with waxed surfaces.
See also Antique Wood, French Polished Wood and Wood, Painted (p. 13).

Artificial flowers (plastic)

General stains: Shake vigorously in salt-filled bag.

Blankets

General stains: *Electric blankets:* Follow manufacturer's care instructions.
Synthetic fibre: Pre-treat spots with heavy duty liquid detergent. Wash, dry-clean or consult professional dry-cleaner.
Woollen blankets: Pre-treat spots by softly brushing with warm Woolite solution. *Or* dry clean. *Or* consult dry-cleaner.
· **Never** use soap, very hot water or water softener on untreated wool blankets. Never wash any blankets unless specified by the manufacturer. Never dry-clean electric blankets.

Books

Grease: Rub with soft, white breadcrumbs.
Mildew: Dust with absorbent powder. Leave 2 days. Brush off.
General stains: Use an art gum eraser.
· **Always** consult professionals with valuable books (see p. 33).
See also Leather.

Candles

General stains: Sponge with methylated spirit.

Candle holders

Wax coated: Freeze for 1 hour. Peel wax off. This does not harm silver.

Cushions

See Pillows (p. 17).

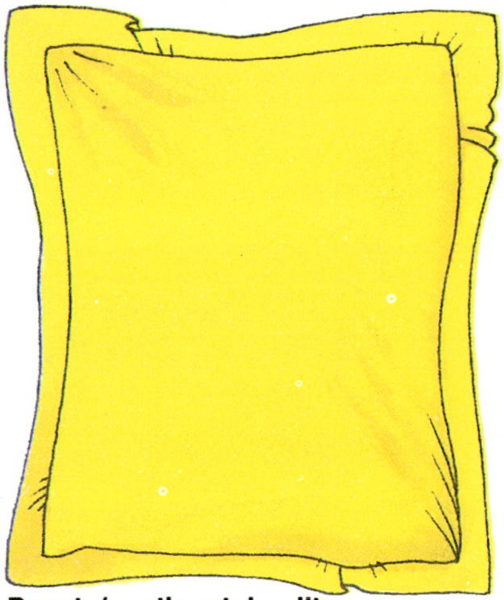

Duvets/continental quilts

Act fast. Treat cover according to stain. See Fabrics (pp. 18–25). If the filling becomes stained—
Natural fibre fillings: Dry-clean or consult specialist cleaner (see p. 33).
Synthetic fibre fillings: Machine wash or consult specialist cleaner (see p. 33).
· **Never** wash too often.
· **Always** follow manufacturer's care instructions. Always use a cover on your duvet, and wash cover according to fabric. Always ensure duvet is dry before use.

Foam rubber

See Pillows, Foam (p. 17).

Frames

General stains: *Gilt:* Wipe with a little white spirit or turpentine. *Or* use liquid dry-cleaner.
Wooden: Wipe with warm soapy water.
· **Never** use harsh abrasives.
· **Always** avoid touching painting.

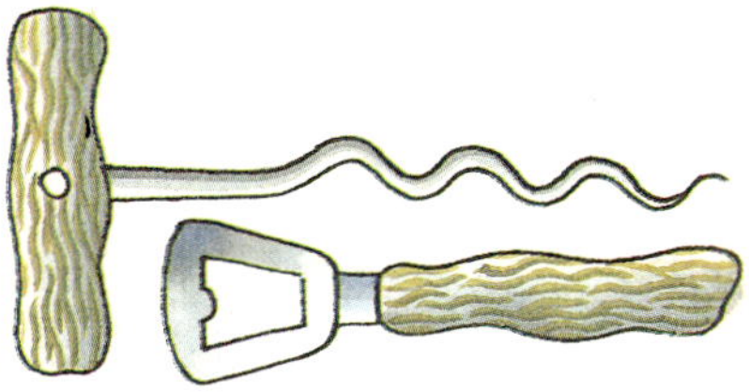

Ivory, bone and horn objects

General stains: Use soft cloth dampened with methylated spirit.
· **Never** use water. Never use methylated spirit on valuable pieces.

Leather

General stains: *Books (binding):* Use leather renovator. Follow instructions.
Clothing/gloves, non-washable: Consult professionals (see p. 33).
Washable: Swab with soapy water. Wipe. Dry naturally. Keep gloves on hands and dip into water. Remove to dry.

Desk/table tops: Rub with leather renovator after washing. **Ink stains:** Rub very gently with a little white spirit.
Luggage/handbags: Rub with eucalyptus oil. Polish with furniture polish.
Shoes: Polish as usual or consult shoe repairer.

Fake leather: Brush gently with warm detergent solution, not soap. Rinse. Buff.
Chamois leather: Wash in warm soapy water. Rinse in warm water plus 1 teaspoon/5 ml olive oil. Squeeze. Dry naturally.
Reptile skin: Rub leather renovator in direction of scales.
Suede, non-washable: Consult professionals (see p. 33).
Washable: Follow manufacturer's care instructions. *Or* use suede cleaner.
Shoes: Brush gently with warm soapy water. Then with cold water. Dry naturally. *Or* use suede cleaner.
· **Never** soak in water (unless chamois). Never use detergent (unless fake leather).
· **Always** follow manufacturer's care instructions.
See also Upholstery, Leather (p. 27).

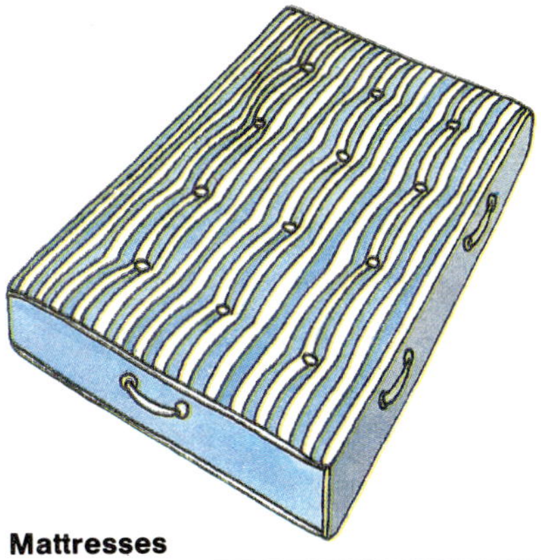

Mattresses

Blood: 1 Tip mattress on side. **2** Sponge with cold, salt water. Rinse with cold water. *Or* use lather from upholstery cleaner.
Urine: 1 Tip mattress on side. **2** Sponge with cold washing-up liquid or upholstery shampoo solution. Rinse with cold water plus disinfectant. *Or* use upholstery spotting kit.
Vomit: 1 Remove deposit. **2** Tip mattress on side. **3** Sponge with warm washing-up liquid or upholstery shampoo solution. **4** Rinse with warm water plus disinfectant. Blot well.
Stubborn stains: Use soap foam. *Or* use upholstery shampoo.
· **Never** expect miracles. Ring marks may remain after cleaning.
· **Always** follow manufacturer's care instructions. Always clean urine stains thoroughly.

Oil paintings

General stains: Consult professional picture restorer if valuable. If not, use a picture cleaner. Follow instructions carefully.
· **Never** attempt to clean valuable paintings.
· **Always** try cleaning a corner first.

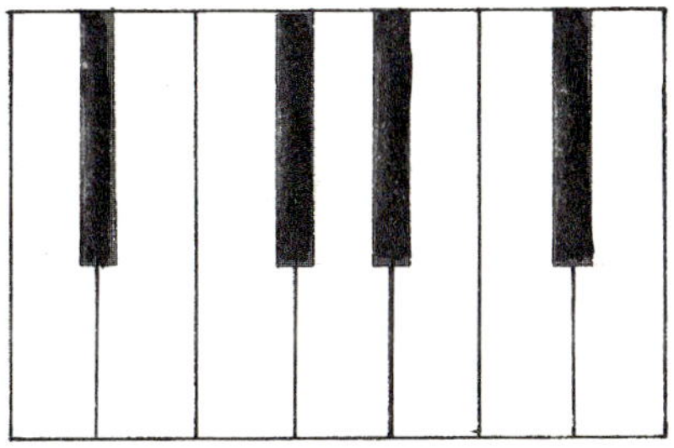

Piano keys

General stains: *Ivory:* If valuable, consult professionals. *Or* use solution (50:50) methylated spirit and warm water. *Or* rub with toothpaste. Buff. Dry.
Plastic: Use warm water plus a few drops of vinegar. Wipe dry.
· **Never** let water get between keys. Never attempt to clean valuable pianos.

Pillows

Act fast. Treat covers according to stain. See Fabrics (pp. 18–25). If the filling becomes stained—
Down and feather: Have professionally washed (see p. 33).
Foam: Wash in warm soapy water. Rinse. Dry thoroughly.
Synthetic fibre: Machine or hand-wash. Follow instructions.
· **Never** dry-clean synthetic fibre pillows. Never use lighter fuel or strong chlorine solution on fabrics encasing foam rubber.
· **Always** use a cover on your pillow and remove and clean it first without touching pillow. Always ensure pillow is completely dry before use.

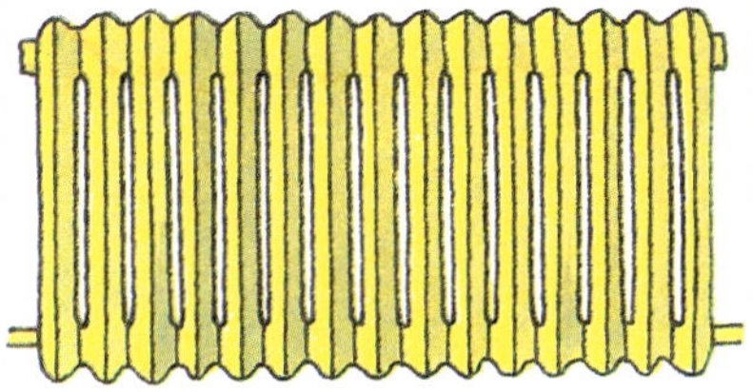

Radiators

See Wood, Painted (p. 13).
· **Always** cover the floor below the radiator when cleaning.

Telephone

General stains: Rub with white spirit.

Fabrics chart

Symbols and Washing Instructions taken from the International Textile Care Labelling Code

Symbol	Machine Wash	Hand Wash	Agitation	Rinse	Spinning	Fabric
1 (95°)	Very hot. 95°C to boil.	Hot. 50°C or boil.	Maximum	Normal	Normal	White cotton and linen without special finishes.
2 (60°)	Hot. 60°C.	Hand hot to 50°C.	Maximum	Normal	Normal	Cotton, linen, modal or viscose (rayon) articles without special finishes where colours are fast at 60°C. Also Denim.
3 (60°)	Hot. 60°C.	Hand hot to 50°C.	Medium	Cold	Short spin or drip-dry.	White nylon, white polyester/cotton mixtures.
4 (50°)	Hand-hot 50°C.	Hand-hot 50°C.	Medium	Cold	Short spin or drip-dry.	Coloured nylon, cotton, polyester, viscose (rayon) with special finishes; acrylic or mod-acrylic and cotton mixtures; coloured cotton and polyester mixtures.
5 (40°)	Warm 40°C.	Warm 40°C.	Medium	Normal	Normal	Cotton, linen or viscose (rayon) articles where colours are fast at 40°C, but not at 60°C. Also Elastane.
6 (40°)	Warm 40°C.	Warm 40°C.	Minimum	Cold	Short spin. Do not hand-wring.	Acrylics, modacrylics; acetate and triacetate, including mixtures with wool; polyester/wool blends.
7 (40°)	Warm 40°C.	Warm 40°C.	Minimum. Do not rub.	Normal	Normal. Do not hand-wring.	Wool, including blankets and wool mixtures with cotton or viscose (rayon); silk.
8 (30°)	Cool 30°C.	Cool 30°C.	Minimum	Cold	Short spin. Do not hand-wring.	Silk and printed acetate fabrics with colours not fast at 40°C.
9 (95°)	Very hot. 95°C to boil.	Hand hot. 50°C or boil.	Minimum	Cold	Drip-dry	Cotton articles with special finishes capable of being boiled but requiring drip-drying.

Symbol		Fabric	Special Instructions
	**Never wash**	Brocade, Silk/Satin/Velvet Felt Fur Leather/Suede Velour Velvet/Velveteen	**Always** have professionally dry-cleaned. **Always** have professionally dry-cleaned. *or* use an absorbent powder. **Always** have professionally dry-cleaned. See Leather (p. 16). **Always** have professionally dry-cleaned. **Always** follow manufacturer's care instructions.
	**Never dry-clean.**	**Polypropylene:** Meraklon.	May be machine-washed in warm water. Do not iron. Follow manufacturer's care instructions.
	**Chlorine bleach may be used.**		

Fibre Generic & Brand Names	Never/Always	Special Instructions	Symbol
	Always wash whites and coloureds separately. Bleaches may be used. Always treat stains before washing. Never use strong acids.	**Linen:** Never use chlorine bleach.	1 95°
Modal: Avril, Vincel, Zantrel, Zaryl. **Viscose (rayon):** Delustra, Evlan, Sarille, Viloft.	Always wash whites and coloureds separately. Bleaches may be used, test first. Always treat stains before washing. Never use acids or strong alkaline solutions.	**Denim:** Always wash separately. Never use bleaches. **Linen:** See above. **Modal/Viscose (rayon):** Never boil.	2 60°
Nylon: Antron, Bri-nylon, Cantrece, Celon, Celon Anti-Stat, Counter-Stat, Cumuloft, Enkacomfort, Enkacrepe, Enkalon, Enkasheer, Enkastat, Miralon, Pavanne, Qiana.	Always wash whites and coloureds separately. Always treat stains before washing.	**Nylon:** Always hand-wash delicate items in cold water. Never use hydrogen peroxide bleach, may use other bleaches.	3 60°
Polyester: Dacron, Diolen, Fortrel, Lirelle, Terlenka, Terylene, Trevira. **Acrylic/Modacrylic:** See below. **Nylon:** See above. **Viscose (rayon):** See above.	Always wash whites and coloured cottons separately. Always follow manufacturer's care label instructions. Always treat stains before washing. Only use bleach on colourfast fabrics. Test first.	**Nylon:** See above. **Viscose (rayon):** Never use methylated/white spirit, acetone, paint brush cleaner or chlorine bleach. Never boil or soak for long. **Acrylic/Modacrylic:** See below.	4 50°
Elastane: Lycra, Spanzelle. **Viscose (rayon):** See above.	Wash white and coloured cottons and linens separately. Always treat stains before washing. Always test before using bleaches. Never use bleaches on non-colourfast fabrics. Test first.	**Viscose (rayon):** See above. **Elastane:** Never use chlorine bleach. Never dry in the sun or artificially.	5 40°
Acetate: Dicel. **Acrylics:** Acrilan, Courtelle, Dralon, Orlon. **Modacrylic:** Acrilan SEF, Kanekalon, Teklan. **Triacetate:** Arnel, Rhonel, Tricel. **Polyester:** See above.	Always follow manufacturer's care instructions. Always treat stains before washing. Always test first before using bleaches.	**Acetate / Acrylic / Modacrylic / Triacetate:** Never use acetone, paint brush cleaner, methylated/white spirit, white vinegar. Always handle acetone gently. Never use bleaches on modacrylics. **Wool:** See below.	6 40°
Wool: Angora, Cashmere. **Viscose (rayon):** See above.	Always follow manufacturer's care instructions. Always treat stains before washing. Always test first before using bleaches.	**Viscose (rayon):** See above. **Silk:** Never use soap, alkalis, ammonia, chlorine bleach or enzyme detergent. Never rub silk, squeeze only. Never dry in the sun or artificially. **Wool:** Never use hydrogen peroxide plus ammonia, or ammonia alone, or alkalies or water-softeners on wool or wool mixtures. Never soak in chlorine bleach or enzyme detergent for long. Always use Woolite and cold water if washing by hand.	7 40°
Acetate: See above.	Always follow manufacturer's care instructions. Always treat stains before washing. Test first before using bleaches.	**Acetate:** See above. **Silk:** See above.	8 30°
	Always follow manufacturer's care instructions. Always treat stains before washing. Always test first before using bleaches. Always wash whites and coloureds separately.		9 95°

Symbol		Fabric	Special Instructions
	**Never machine wash**	Canvas	Wipe with a damp cloth or scrub with soap lather. Never over-wet.
		Wool, Cashmere, Angora	**Always** follow manufacturer's care instructions. May be machine-washed, but it is advisable not to do so.
		Fur Fabric	**Always** follow manufacturer's care instructions. May be dry-cleaned professionally.
		Lace	**Antique:** Soak in cold distilled water. *Or* consult professionals. **Machine-made:** See Nylon/Polyester.
		Metallic Fibres (Lurex)	Follow manufacturer's care instructions.
		PVC	Wipe clean with a damp cloth. Treat stains at once.
	**Never use chlorine bleach**		**Never** use on linen, non-colourfast fabrics, viscose, elastane, modacrylic, wool, silk. **Never** use on crease-resistant, drip-dry, embossed or piqué fabrics. Always test first.

Cleaning methods

1 Dry-cleaning method

Referred to in the text as **Method 1**.

Stain removal: 1 Remove surface deposit. **2** If possible put clean white cotton wool or similar absorbent pad under fabric with wrong side of fabric facing upwards. **3** Dab, not rub, carefully with another clean pad saturated with the recommended dry-cleaning solvent. **4** Blot dry after each application. **5** Launder or dry-clean as usual.

Never
- pour cleaning agents directly onto surface.
- over-wet fabric with cleaning agent or rub too hard.
- let cleaning agents touch rubber-latexed or foam-backed carpets.

Always
- consult Fabrics Chart (pp. 18–19) and follow manufacturer's instructions if available.
- consult Cleaning Agents (pp. 2–3) and follow label instructions carefully.
- test cleaning agent on hidden part of fabric before using. Wait 15 minutes. If fabric is damaged, seek professional advice.
- use repeated weak applications of cleaning agent, not one strong one.
- work from the outside towards the centre of the stain to avoid making rings.
- change pads frequently.
- seek professional advice if the stain persists.

2 Absorbent method

Referred to in the text as **Method 2**.

Stain removal: 1 Remove surface deposit. **2** Spread the fabric as flat as possible. **3** Apply absorbent powder thickly over stain and flatten gently. **4** Remove when saturated and re-apply as necessary. *Or* leave one hour and remove.

Never
- use absorbent powders on carpets.

Always
- consult Cleaning Agents (pp. 2–3) and follow label instructions carefully.
- seek professional advice if stain persists.

3 Sponging and soaking method (fabrics)

Referred to in the text as **Method 3**.

Stain removal: *Non-washable fabrics:* **1** Remove surface deposit. **2** Use cold water and sponge gently. **3** When possible, pour cold water from height of 2–3 feet in through stained part of fabric after stretching over bowl.

Always
- consult Fabrics Chart (pp. 18–19) and follow manufacturer's care instructions if available.
- consult Cleaning Agents (pp. 2–3) and follow label instructions carefully.
- test cleaning agent on hidden part of fabric before using.

Stain removal: *Washable fabrics:* **1** Remove surface deposit. Act fast. **2** Rinse with cold or warm water. **3** Soak in solution of cleaning agent recommended. If stain persists, put clean white cotton wool or similar absorbent pad under fabric with wrong side of fabric on top. **4** Sponge with cleaning solution on another clean pad. **5** Rinse with clear water. Blot dry. **6** Repeat if necessary.

Never
- soak wool, silk, non-colourfast or flame-proof fabrics.

Always
- consult Fabrics Chart (pp. 18–19) and follow manufacturer's care instructions if available.
- consult Cleaning Agents (pp. 2–3) and follow label instructions carefully.
- test cleaning agent on hidden part of fabric before using. Then place wet fabric between two white cloths. Apply warm iron. If cloths remain unmarked, fabric is colourfast. If non-colourfast, seek professional advice.

4 Sponging and soaking method (upholstery and carpets)

Referred to in the text as **Method 4**.

Stain removal: 1 Use foam shampoo or dissolve upholstery or liquid carpet shampoo in warm water until it foams. **2** Sponge stain lightly with foam. Blot often. **3** Rinse with cold water by sponging gently. **4** If stain persists leave to dry then use **Method 1** (see above). *Or* seek professional advice. *Or* for small stains, use a spotting kit or spot remover. Follow instructions.

Never
- over-wet fabric/carpet.
- use household detergent on upholstery.
- use soap, soap powder or soda on carpets.

Always
- consult Fabrics Chart (pp. 18–19) and follow manufacturer's care instructions if available.
- consult Cleaning Agents (pp. 2–3) and follow label instructions carefully.
- test cleaning agent on hidden part of fabric/carpet before using. If fabric/carpet is damaged seek professional advice.
- use lather only if using detergent on carpets. Dry carpet outside if possible or else lift clear of floor to dry.

5 Boiling water method (white and colourfast linens only)

Referred to in the text as **Method 5**.

Stain removal: 1 Stretch fabric over basin. **2** Sprinkle stain with a little detergent or dry borax. **3** Pour boiling water through stained part of fabric from height of 2–3 feet. Rinse. **4** If stain persists, see **Method 1** *or* **Method 3** *or* **4.**

6 Bleaching method

Referred to in the text as **Method 6**.

Never
- use on carpets or upholstery.

Always
- consult Fabrics Chart (pp. 18–19) and follow manufacturer's care instructions if available.
- consult Cleaning Agents (pp. 2–3) and follow label instructions carefully.
- test cleaning agents on a hidden part of fabric before using.

First aid (fabrics, including upholstery)

1 Act fast. The faster you act the milder the remedy needed.
2 Blot dry. *Or* remove surface deposit.
3 **Grease stains:** Cover with an absorbent powder.
Fruit/wine/beetroot stains: Cover with salt.
Other stains: Rinse with cold water.
4 Always follow manufacturer's care instructions if available.
5 Find relevant stain in Fabrics (pp. 21-25) or Upholstery (pp. 26-27) Sections. Read relevant section of Cleaning Methods (p. 20) and follow instructions carefully.
6 If necessary test cleaning agent first in an inconspicuous place.
7 Be cautious. If in doubt or unable to identify stain consult professionals.
8 Once stain is treated, dry quickly and evenly with hair-dryer or fan heater to prevent ring appearing, unless otherwise mentioned.
9 After treating stain launder or dry-clean as usual for best results.
10 If the stain persists consult professionals.

Always refer to First aid (above) and Cleaning methods (p. 20) before taking action.

Animal stains: See Urine/Vomit.
Bird droppings: **1** Soak. **2** If necessary use hydrogen peroxide/bleach solution. Not on nylon (Method 6). *Or* use dry-cleaner (Method 1).

Blood, *Washable fabrics:* **1** Soak immediately in cold water (Method 3). **2** Wash in warm enzyme detergent solution or upholstery shampoo (Method 3). *Or* soak in hydrogen peroxide solution (Method 6). For dried stains use ammonia (Method 3). Then wash as above.
Non-washable fabrics: **1** Wipe or brush off surplus. **2** Sponge with cold water plus few drops ammonia (Method 3). Rinse. Blot well. *Or* use upholstery spotting kit. **3** If necessary, sponge with hydrogen peroxide plus ammonia (Method 3). Leave 10 minutes. Rinse.
Cologne: See Perfume.
Cosmetics: See Foundation cream, Lipstick.

Deodorant: **1** Soak in white vinegar or ammonia solution (Method 3). **2** If necessary, use methylated spirit (Method 1).
Droppings: See Vomit.
Foundation cream, *Washable fabrics:* **1** Remove deposit. **2** Soak in ammonia solution (Method 3). Rinse. **3** Launder. **Dried stains:** **1** Brush off excess. **2** Loosen with glycerine solution. Rinse. **3** Wash.
Non-washable fabrics: **1** Remove deposit. **2** Use dry-cleaner (Method 1). *Or* use absorbent powder (Method 2). *Or* use upholstery spotting kit.
Hair oil/cream: See Grease (p. 24).
Hair spray: Either sponge with cold water *or* use methylated spirit/acetone/amyl acetate (Method 1).

Indelible lipstick: **1** Rub with lard. **2** Use dry-cleaner (Method 1).
Lipstick: **1** Sponge with eucalyptus oil or glycerine. Rinse. **2** Use lighter fuel or dry-cleaner (Method 1).
Mascara: Use dry-cleaner (Method 1).

Perfume: **1** Sponge with water at once. **2** Use glycerine solution. Rinse. **3** Launder if possible. Have delicate fabrics dry-cleaned professionally.
Perspiration: Sponge with warm enzyme detergent solution (Method 3). *Or* use ammonia solution. **Old stains:** **1** Use white vinegar solution (Method 3). **2** If necessary, use hydrogen peroxide/chlorine bleach solution (Method 6) *or* dry-cleaner (Method 1).

Sun-tan oil: Soak or sponge with enzyme detergent solution (Method 3).
Sweat: See Perspiration.
Urine: *Washable fabrics:* **1** Rinse in cold water. **2** Launder as normal. **Dried stains:** **1** Soak in enzyme detergent solution (Method 3). **2** Use hydrogen peroxide plus ammonia solution if necessary (Method 6).
Non-washable fabrics: **1** Sponge with cold water. **2** Sponge with white vinegar solution (Method 3). Have dried stains dry-cleaned professionally.
Vomit: *Washable fabrics:* **1** Remove deposit. **2** Rinse with cold running water. **3** Soak in enzyme detergent solution (Method 3). **4** Launder as normal.
Non-washable fabrics: **1** Remove deposit. **2** Sponge with ammonia solution (Method 3) *or* use upholstery spotting kit. **3** If necessary, have dry-cleaned professionally.

Always refer to First aid and Cleaning methods (pp. 20-21) before taking action.

Alcohol: **1** Wipe up immediately. **2** Sponge with warm water. **3** Wash or sponge with liquid detergent solution (Method 3 or 4). Rinse with warm water. *Or* use an upholstery spotting kit (Method 4). **4** If necessary, use chlorine/hydrogen peroxide bleach (Method 6).

Baked beans: **1** Soak in enzyme detergent (Method 3). **2** Use dry-cleaner (Method 1).

Beer: *Washable fabrics:* For dried stains on white cottons/linens, use hydrogen peroxide solution (Method 6). For dried stains on coloured fabrics sponge with white vinegar (Method 3).

Non-washable fabrics: Use detergent or carpet shampoo (Method 3 or 4). For dried stains sponge with white vinegar solution (Method 3). *Or* use dry-cleaner. *Or* an upholstery spotting kit.

Beetroot: Soak in enzyme detergent solution (Method 3).

Bottled sauces: See Ketchup.

Butter: See Grease (p. 24).

Chewing gum: **1** Chill with ice cube to harden. **2** Scrape off. **3** Use dry-cleaner (Method 1). **4** Wash or sponge with warm water. *Or* use Chewing gum remover.

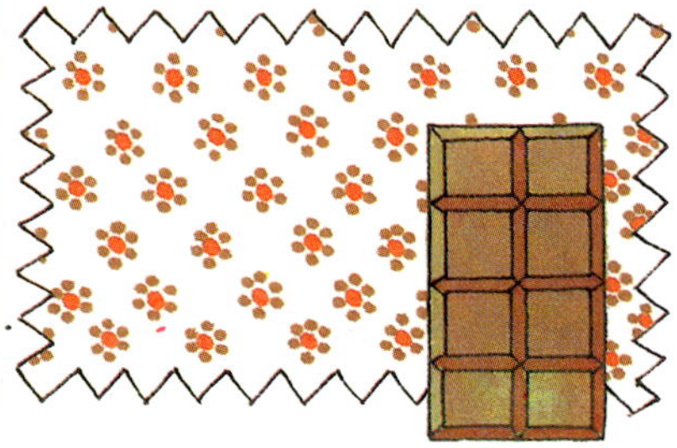

Chocolate/cocoa: **1** Scrape off deposit. **2** Use enzyme detergent or borax solution (Method 3). *Or* use boiling water from height (Method 5). **3** If stain persists, and for non-washable fabrics, use dry-cleaner (Method 1).

Chutney: See Jam.

Cod-liver oil: *Washable fabrics:* Wash immediately in detergent solution. Dried stains: **1** Use dry-cleaner (Method 1). **2** If marks remain, lubricate with glycerine solution. Rinse. **3** Launder as usual. **4** If necessary, use hydrogen peroxide solution (Method 6).

Non-washable fabrics: Use dry-cleaner (Method 1).

Woollens: Sponge immediately with mild detergent solution. Wash. **Dried stains:** use liquid stain remover (Method 1). Wash. Impossible to remove old stains.

Coffee: **1** Sponge with borax solution (Method 3). Loosen dried stains with glycerine solution. **2** Use chlorine bleach (Method 6) if necessary. *Or* on certain fabrics, pour boiling water from height (Method 5), using borax if necessary.

Dralon: Sponge with warm enzyme detergent solution. Rub lightly in the direction of the pile. Do not over-wet.

Cream: *Washable fabrics:* **1** Use enzyme detergent or borax (Method 3). **2** When dry, use dry-cleaner (Method 1).

Non-washable fabrics: **1** Use dry-cleaner (Method 1). **2** Sponge carefully with cold water.

Curry: *Washable fabrics:* **1** Remove deposit. **2** Soften with glycerine solution. **3** Use enzyme detergent or ammonia solution (Method 3). **4** Bleach if necessary (Method 6).

Non-washable fabrics: **1** Remove deposit. **2** Use ammonia or borax solution (Method 1). **3** If necessary, have professionally dry-cleaned.

Egg: *Washable fabrics:* **1** Scrape off deposit. **2** Sponge or soak with cold salt water. **3** Use enzyme detergent solution (Method 3). **4** Use an aerosol dry-cleaner to remove any traces.

Non-washable fabrics: **1** Remove deposit. **2** Sponge with cold salt water. **3** When dry use dry-cleaner (Method 1).

Fats: See Grease (p. 24).

Fish slime: **1** Soak or sponge with salt water. Rinse. **2** Wash as usual.

Fruit/fruit juice: *Washable fabrics:* **1** Sponge or soak immediately in cold salt water or milk. **2** If necessary, sponge with white vinegar or use hydrogen peroxide (Method 6). **Dried stains:** **1** Loosen with glycerine solution. **2** Soak in enzyme detergent solution (Method 3).
Non-washable fabrics: **1** Sponge with cold water. **2** When dry, use dry-cleaner (Method 1). *Or* use upholstery spotting kit.
White and colourfast linens: **1** Cover stain with salt. **2** Use boiling water (Method 5) plus borax. *Or* use colour and stain remover.

Gravy: *Washable fabrics:* **1** Remove deposit. **2** Sponge or soak with cold water. **3** Use dry-cleaner (Method 1). **Dried stains:** **1** Soak in enzyme detergent solution (Method 3). **2** Wash.
Non-washable fabrics: **1** Remove deposit. **2** Sponge with cold water. *Or* apply absorbent powder (Method 2). *Or* use dry-cleaner (Method 1).
Honey: Soak or sponge with enzyme detergent solution (Method 3). *Or* use dry-cleaner (Method 1).
Ice cream: See Cream.
Ice lolly: **1** Soak or sponge with enzyme detergent solution (Method 3). **2** Use hydrogen peroxide (Method 6) if necessary.

Jam/marmalade: **1** Remove deposit. **2** Sponge or soak with liquid detergent/ enzyme detergent/borax solution (Method 3). **3** If necessary, use chlorine bleach (Method 6) *or* dry-cleaner (Method 1).
Juice: See Fruit.

Ketchup/bottled sauces: *Washable fabrics:* **1** Remove deposit. **2** Sponge with cold liquid detergent solution. Rinse. **3** Soak in enzyme detergent solution (Method 3).
Non-washable fabrics: **1** Remove deposit. **2** Wipe with cold water. **3** Use dry-cleaner (Method 1) when dry. **4** If necessary, have dry-cleaned professionally.
Liqueurs: See Alcohol.
Margarine: See Cream.
Marmalade: See Jam.
Mayonnaise: See Cream.
Milk: **1** Sponge or soak in cold water. **2** Launder as normal. **3** If necessary, use upholstery spotting kit *or* dry-cleaner (Method 1).

Mustard: **1** Sponge or soak in mild detergent solution. **2** Use ammonia solution on remaining stain (Method 3). **3** Launder if possible. *Or* sponge with hydrogen peroxide (Method 1) on suitable fabrics. Have fabrics that ring mark easily dry-cleaned professionally.
Salad dressing: See Cream.
Sauces: See Cream.
Soft drinks: See Fruit Juice.
Soup: See Ketchup.
Spirits: See Alcohol.
Syrup: See Jam.

Tea: See Coffee. *Or* use an absorbent powder (Method 2).

Tomato juice: See Fruit.
Treacle: See Jam.
Turmeric: See Curry.
Vinegar: **1** Soak or sponge in enzyme detergent solution (Method 3). **2** Launder if possible. **3** If the colour of the fabric has been affected, see Acids (p. 24).

Wine: *Washable fabrics:* **1** Squirt with soda syphon. *Or* saturate red wine stain with white wine. *Or* cover with salt, rub off when dry. **2** Use boiling water from height (Method 5). *Or* soak in borax or enzyme detergent solution (Method 3). **3** If necessary, use dry-cleaner (Method 1) *or* hydrogen peroxide (Method 6).
Non-washable fabrics: Act fast. **1** Sponge with warm water. *Or* blot stain and cover with absorbent powder (Method 2). Repeat as necessary. **2** Use glycerine solution on dried stains. **3** Sponge with warm detergent solution (Method 3), rinse. *Or* use an upholstery spotting kit.
Yoghurt: **1** Remove deposit. **2** Use dry-cleaner (Method 1).
Zabaglione: **1** Remove deposit. **2** Use dry-cleaner (Method 1). *Or* soak in enzyme detergent solution (Method 3) where possible.

Always refer to First aid and Cleaning methods (pp. 20-21) before taking action.

Acids (sulphuric/hydrochloric/acetic/vinegar): 1 Use cold water (Method 3). **2** Sponge with ammonia or bicarbonate of soda solution (1 teaspoon/5 ml to 1 cup/ 225 ml water). Rinse. Strong acids may cause permanent damage.

Adhesives: Some now have their own special solvents which may be obtained from the manufacturer. Follow instructions.

Adhesive tape (Sellotape): Use dry-cleaner (Method 1).

Clear and contact adhesives (Bostik/Evo-Stik): 1 Use non-oily nail varnish remover, acetone or amyl acetate (Method 1). **2** If necessary use bleach (Method 6).

Epoxy resin (Araldite): Use acetone, amyl acetate or cellulose thinners. On synthetic fibres use lighter fuel (Method 1). Stains cannot be removed once dry.

Latex adhesive (Copydex): If wet: remove with a damp cloth. If dry: **1** Scrape off surplus. **2** Use dry-cleaner or paint brush cleaner (Method 1). *Or* use manufacturer's solvent.

Model-making cement: 1 Wipe off surplus. **2** Use dry-cleaner or amyl acetate (Method 1). Stains cannot be removed when dry.

Alkalies (ammonia/washing soda): 1 Sponge immediately with cold water. **2** Use lemon juice or white vinegar or developer solution (Method 1). Strong alkalies may cause permanent damage.

Ballpoint: See Ink.

Battery acids: See Acids.

Burns: See Scorch Marks.

Candle wax: 1 Scrape off deposit. **2** Place blotting paper over (and under if possible) fabric and press quickly with a warm iron, repeat until wax is absorbed. Change paper often. **3** Remove colour traces with methylated spirit or dry-cleaner (Method 1). **4** If necessary, use chlorine bleach (Method 6). Rinse. *Or* pour boiling water from height through strong fabrics (Method 5).

Carbon paper: See Transfer Pattern.

Crayon: Use dry-cleaner or lighter fuel (Method 1).

Creosote: Use eucalyptus oil/lighter fuel/ dry-cleaner (Method 1).

Duplicating ink: See Ink.

Dyes: *Washable fabrics:* **1** Soak in enzyme detergent solution (Method 3). **2** If necessary use chlorine bleach or hydrogen peroxide (Method 6). *Or* use colour and stain remover.

Non-washable fabrics: Use methylated spirit plus a few drops of ammonia (Method 1).

Felt-tip: See Ink.

Flower stains: See Grass.

Glue: See Adhesives.

Grass: 1 Use eucalyptus oil/glycerine/ methylated spirit (Method 1). Rinse. *Or* use equal parts of cream of tartar and salt (Method 2). Remove after 10 minutes. **2** If necessary use dry-cleaner (Method 1). *Or* chlorine bleach/hydrogen peroxide (Method 6).

Grease: *Washable fabrics:* **1** Remove deposit. **2** Use absorbent powder (Method 2). *Or* use blotting paper and warm iron (see Candle Wax). **3** Wash in warm soapflake solution (Method 3). **4** If necessary use dry-cleaner (Method 1).

Non-washable fabrics: **1** Scrape off deposit. **2** Use absorbent or warm iron method (See above). **3** Use dry-cleaner (Method 1) if necessary. **Heavy stains:** Use paint brush cleaner (Method 1).

Ink, ballpoint/felt tip: 1 Use methylated spirit (Method 1). *Or* use glycerine with ammonia solution (Method 1). Keep moist. Blot often. **2** If necessary use chlorine bleach solution (Method 6) *or* dry-cleaner (Method 1).

Polyester: Spray ballpoint stain with hair spray. Rub off with clean cloth.

Ink, Indian: Act fast. **1** Soak or sponge with cold water. **2** Wash with liquid detergent/ soapflake solution. **3** Soak or sponge in ammonia solution (Method 3). Rinse. **4** If colour is affected sponge with white vinegar. **5** If necessary, consult professionals.

Ink, printing: Sponge with turpentine (Method 1).

Ink, writing: *Washable fabrics:* **1** Sponge or soak with cold water or milk. **2** Use enzyme detergent solution (Method 3). **3** If necessary, use dry-cleaner (Method 1). *Or* use chlorine bleach/hydrogen peroxide solution (Method 6). **4** If yellow stains remain, see Rust.

Non-washable fabrics: **1** Use absorbent powder (Method 2). **2** Sponge with enzyme detergent solution *or* dry-cleaner. See Washable above.

Iodine: *Washable fabrics:* **1** Sponge or soak immediately in water. **2** Sponge in detergent solution (Method 3). *Or* have dry-cleaned professionally.

Non-washable fabrics: Use alcohol (Method 1). *Or* have dry-cleaned professionally.

Iron rust: See Rust.

Lead pencil: 1 Use an india rubber/eraser. **2** Use dry-cleaner or methylated spirit (Method 1) if necessary.

Medicine, iron-based: See Rust.
Medicine, syrup-based: Wash or sponge with soapy solution (Method 3).
Medicine, tar-based: 1 Rub with vaseline or lard. **2** Use dry-cleaner (Method 1). **3** If any colour remains, use methylated spirit (Method 1). *Or* have professionally dry-cleaned.
Metal polish: 1 Remove deposit. **2** Use white spirit or lighter fuel (Method 1). **3** Use dry-cleaner (Method 1).
Mildew: *Washable fabrics:* **1** Moisten with lemon/lime juice and salt. Dry in the sun. *Or* use hard soap or enzyme detergent solution (Method 3). Dry in the sun. **2** If necessary, use hydrogen peroxide/chlorine bleach solution (Method 6).
Non-washable fabrics: Have dry-cleaned professionally.
Mud: 1 Remove deposit. **2** Sponge or soak with cold water or mild detergent solution (Method 3). Rinse. **Dried stains: 1** Brush. **2** Use dry-cleaner (Method 1) if necessary.

Nail varnish: 1 Remove deposit. **2** Use amyl acetate or non-oily nail varnish remover (Method 1). **3** Use methylated spirit (Method 1) if necessary.

Nicotine: Use eucalyptus oil or methylated spirit (Method 1). *Or* soak in enzyme detergent solution (Method 3). *Or* hydrogen peroxide (Method 6).
Oil: 1 Use absorbent powder (Method 2). **2** Use dry-cleaner (Method 1) if necessary. *Or* cover with a paste of sugar and water before laundering.

Paint, oil-based: 1 Remove deposit. **2** Sponge with white spirit/turpentine/paint brush cleaner (Method 1). Test first. **3** Sponge with cold water. **4** Launder if possible.
Paint, water-based: 1 Remove deposit. **2** Sponge with cold water. **3** Launder if possible. **Dried paint:** Use methylated spirit or paint brush cleaner (Method 1).
Paraffin: See Candle Wax.
Pencil: See Lead Pencil.
Plasticine: 1 Remove deposit. **2** Use dry-cleaner or lighter fuel (Method 1) on small areas. Test first. **3** Launder if possible.
Resins: See Creosote.
Rust: *Washable fabrics:* Rub with lemon/lime juice and salt. Dry in the sun. *Or* rub with lemon/lime juice and hold in the steam from a kettle for 2 minutes. *Or* boil in solution 1 pint/500 ml water, 4 tablespoons/60 ml cream of tartar (Method 3). Rinse. *Or* use rust remover.
Non-washable fabrics: Have cleaned professionally.
Sand: 1 Brush off excess. **2** Soak or sponge in enzyme detergent solution (Method 3). **3** Use hydrogen peroxide/chlorine bleach (Method 6).

Scorch marks: *Washable fabrics:* Soak in borax/hydrogen peroxide/ammonia solution (Method 3). Rinse. May be impossible to remove from silk or wool or if the cloth fibres have been burnt.
Non-washable fabrics: **1** Rub with glycerine solution. Rinse. **2** If necessary, sponge with borax solution (Method 3 or 4).
Shellac: Act fast. **1** Use dry-cleaner or methylated spirit (Method 1). **2** Launder if possible.

Shoe polish: *Washable fabrics:* **1** Remove deposit. **2** Use dry-cleaner or white spirit (Method 1). **3** Soak in ammonia solution (Method 3). **4** Launder as usual.
Non-washable fabrics: **1** Remove deposit. **2** Use white spirit/turpentine/dry-cleaner (Method 1). **3** Use methylated spirit (Method 1) if necessary. If turpentine or white spirit is used, sponge with warm detergent solution afterwards.
Smoke and soot: *Washable fabrics:* **1** Vacuum deposit. **2** Soak in enzyme detergent solution (Method 3). **3** Launder as usual.
Non-washable fabrics: **1** Vacuum deposit. **2** Use an absorbent powder (Method 2). **3** Vacuum again. **4** Use dry-cleaner (Method 1). If the stain is large, have dry-cleaned professionally.
Soap: Re-wash article and rinse thoroughly.
Tar: *Washable fabrics:* **1** Remove deposit. **2** Use eucalyptus oil (Method 1). **3** Launder as usual.
Non-washable fabrics: **1** Remove deposit. **2** Use glycerine solution. Rinse. **3** If necessary, use dry-cleaner/turpentine/lighter fuel (Method 1).
Tobacco: See Grass.
Transfer patterns: Use methylated spirit or dry-cleaner (Method 1).
Unidentified stains: Have dry-cleaned professionally.
Varnish: See Shellac. If cellulose or polyurethane, see Paint.
Water spots: Hold items in the steam from a boiling kettle. *Or* have dry-cleaned professionally.
Wax: See Candle Wax.

Bedspreads

See Fabrics (pp. 18–25).

Blinds, canvas roller/Roman

Light spots: Use soft india rubber.
Rips/tears: Mend with clear nail varnish.
General stains: *Washable fabrics:* **1** Scrub with warm soapy water. **2** Rinse in cold water. Dry naturally.
Non-washable fabrics: Rub with flour on rough flannel cloth.

Blinds, Venetian

General stains: *Painted/plastic:* Wash one slat at a time with mild soapy water using a cloth. *Or* use paintwork cleaner. *Or* use white spirit on a soft cloth.
Natural wood: Clean one slat at a time with liquid furniture polish. Change cloth frequently.
· **Always** rinse and dry painted and plastic blinds carefully.

Curtains

· **Never** machine wash, tub, twist or mangle fibreglass curtains. Never iron fibreglass curtains. Never dry-clean fibreglass curtains. Never iron plastic curtains. Never soak rayon curtains.
· **Always** follow manufacturer's care instructions. Always test first. Always remove hooks, curtain weights etc. from curtains before washing. Always wear rubber gloves when washing fibreglass curtains. Always hand-wash delicate fabrics.
See also Fabrics (pp. 18–25).

Upholstery, fabric/textile

· **Never** over-wet. Never use household detergent. Never use methylated spirit on acetate or triacetate, modacrylic or rayon upholstery.
· **Always** use a clean cloth. Always test first. Always follow manufacturer's care instructions. Always check on properties of fabric before starting cleaning.
Adhesives: See Adhesives (p. 24).
Alcohol: See Alcohol (p. 22).
Animal stains: See Urine/Vomit.
Ballpoint: See Ink.

Beer: See Beer (p. 22).
Blood: Rub lightly with paste of cornflour and cold water. Leave to dry. Brush off. Repeat.

Burns: See Scorch Marks (p. 25).
Butter: See Grease.
Candle wax: **1** Remove deposit. **2** Cover with blotting paper. Press with warm iron. Repeat until absorbed. Change paper often. **3** Remove colour traces with methylated spirit or dry-cleaner (Method 1).

Chewing gum: See Chewing Gum (p. 22).
Chocolate: **1** Remove deposit. **2** Use dry-cleaner (Method 1).

Chutney, cocoa, coffee, crayon, cream, curry, dyes, egg, fruit, fruit juice, glue, grass, gravy: See Fabrics (pp. 21–25).
Grease: Use salt or cornflour (Method 2). Brush off once grease is absorbed.
Hair oil cream: Use dry-cleaner (Method 1).
Honey: See Honey (p. 30).

Ice cream: See Cream (p. 23).
Ink, ballpoint: Use methylated spirit (Method 1). *Or* consult dry cleaner.
Ink, felt tip: See Ballpoint. *Or* use dry-cleaner (Method 1).

Ink, fountain pen: Act fast. Use cold water or lemon juice (Method 1). Blot. *Or* use upholstery spotting kit.
Jam/marmalade, ketchup, lead pencil, lipstick, mayonnaise, metal polish, mildew, milk, mud, nail varnish: See Fabrics (pp. 21–25).
Oil: See Grease.
Paint, Plasticine, rust: See Fabrics (p. 25).
Salad dressing: See Grease.
Sauces: See Cream (p. 22).

Scorch marks, shoe polish, smoke and soot, soft drinks, soup, spirits, syrup, tar, tea, tomato juice, treacle: See Fabrics (pp. 21–25).
Spirits: See Alcohol (p. 22).
Urine/vomit: **1** Remove deposit. Blot. **2** Use dry-cleaner (Method 1). **3** If possible rinse under cold running water.
Wax: See Candle Wax.

Wine: See Wine (p. 23).

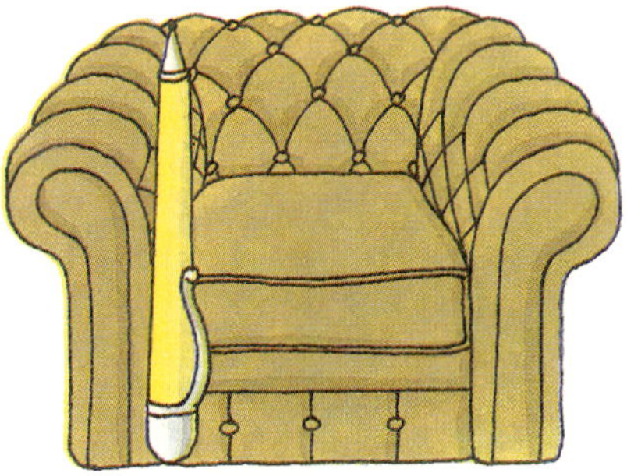

Upholstery, leather

Ballpoint: Sponge immediately with milk.
Cracking leather: Apply solution of 1 part vinegar, 2 parts linseed oil regularly.
Ink: Sponge immediately with water.
General stains: Use soft cloth moistened with soapflake solution. *Or* use a damp cloth rubbed over a bar of glycerine soap.

· **Never** use detergent. Never rinse after washing with soap. Never use dry-cleaning fluid, petrol or ammonia.
· **Always** consult professional upholstery cleaner on non-washable leather.
See also Leather (p. 16).

Upholstery, tapestry

· **Always** have dry-cleaned professionally.

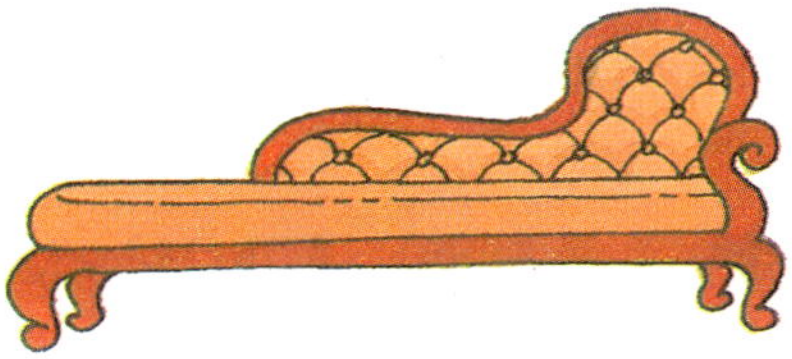

Upholstery, velvet/velveteen

· **Always** have dry-cleaned professionally.

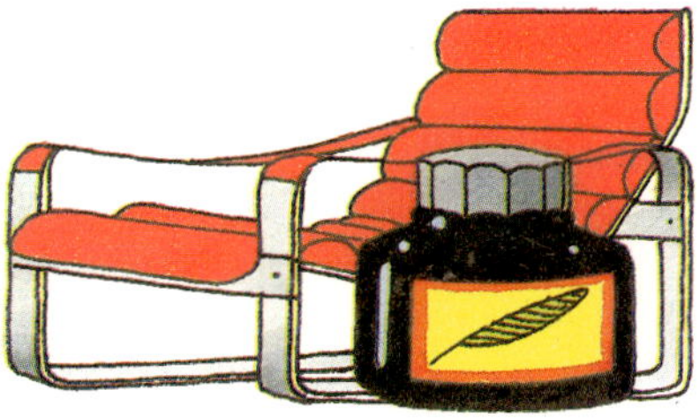

Upholstery, vinyl and other plastics

Ballpoint: Consult dry cleaner.
Chewing gum: **1** Scrape off deposit. **2** Use paraffin or lighter fuel and rub with soft cloth.
Ink: Wipe at once with water or alcohol.
Nail varnish and nail varnish remover: **1** Remove instantly. **2** Blot carefully. Avoid spreading.
Paint and shoe polish: Wipe immediately. Rub with turpentine.

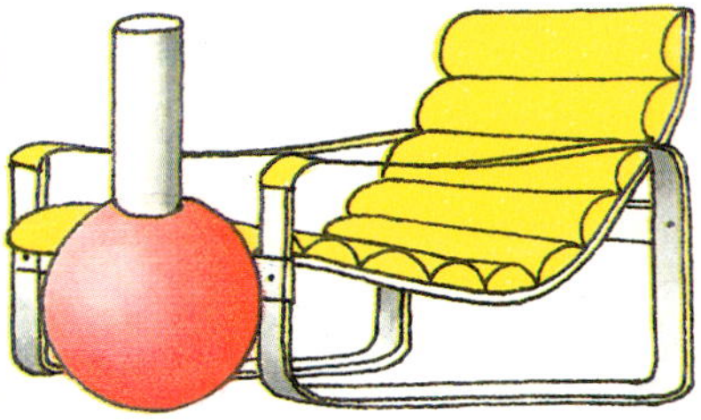

Tar, asphalt and road oil: Remove immediately with turpentine or lighter fuel.
General stains: Wipe with warm soapy water. Rinse with clean damp cloth. Buff. *Or* use a vinyl upholstery cleaner. *Or* use bicarbonate of soda or vinegar on rough, damp cloth. Wash with warm soapy water.
· **Never** over-wet. Never use harsh chemicals, solvents or spirit cleaners. Never use wax polishes.
· **Always** act fast. Always test first.
See also Vinyl Flooring (p. 11) and Vinyl Wallcoverings (p. 13).

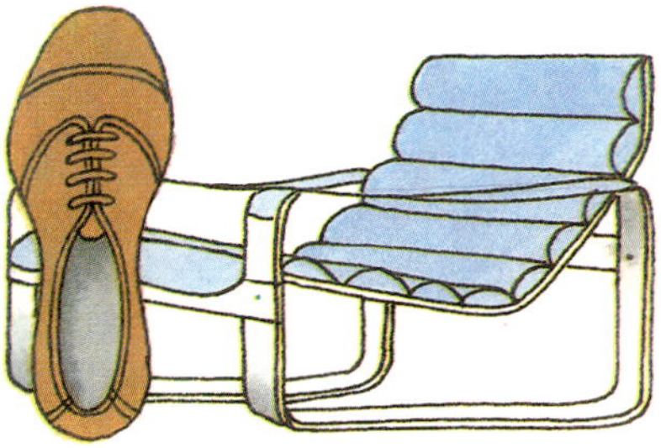

Upholstery, water repellant fabrics

· **Always** have dry-cleaned professionally *or* follow manufacturer's care instructions.

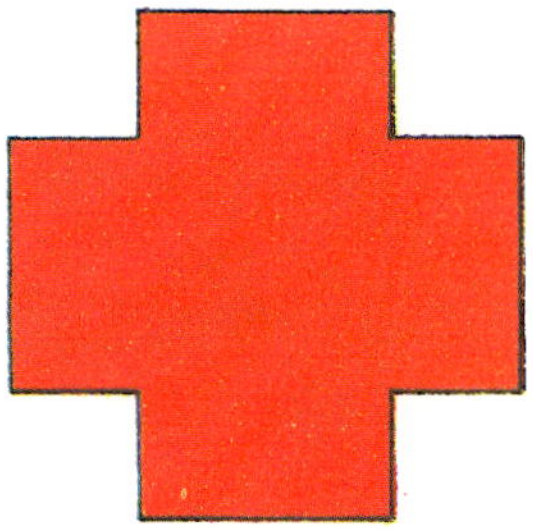

First aid

1 Act fast. The faster you act the milder the remedy needed.
2 Blot liquids. *Or* remove surface deposit. Then flood the stain with soda syphon or cold water. Blot.
3 Always follow manufacturer's care instructions if available.
4 Check carpet fibre and consult Carpets Section (below) for advice on various carpet fibres.
5 Find relevant stain in Carpets (pp. 28-30). Read relevant section of Clean-Methods (p. 20) and follow instructions carefully.
6 Test cleaning agent first in an inconspicuous place.
7 Always blot dry before and after using dry-cleaners.
8 Be cautious. If in doubt or unable to identify stain consult professionals.
9 After treating stain shampoo whole carpet for best results.
10 If stain persists consult professionals.

Types of carpets and rugs

Acrylic and modacrylic carpets
· **Never** use acetone, paint brush cleaner, methylated spirit or white spirit.

Dhurries (Indian cotton rugs)
· **Always** remove from floor immediately and have professionally cleaned.

Felt carpets
· **Always** have professionally cleaned.

Fur/shaggy rugs
· **Always** have professionally cleaned.

Oriental/antique rugs
· **Always** have professionally cleaned.

Rush/sisal matting
Act fast.
Grease: Use aerosol dry-cleaner (Method 1).
Non-greasy stains: Use carpet shampoo (Method 4).
· **Never** over-wet. Never use detergents, ammonia, washing soda, strong alkalies or household soap.
· **Always** follow manufacturer's care instructions.

Skin rugs
· **Always** have professionally cleaned.

Woollen carpets
· **Never** use ammonia.

Always refer to Cleaning methods and check Carpet type before taking action.

Acids: See Acids (p. 24).
Adhesives: See Adhesives (p. 24). If stains are indelible, trim carpet with scissors.
Animal stains: See Urine/Vomit.
Ballpoint: See Ink.

Battery acid: Act fast. Blot. Apply weak solution of borax (Method 4). Be careful.
Blood: Act fast. Flush with soda syphon or cold water. Blot. *Or* use carpet spotting kit (Method 4). Difficult to remove dried stains.

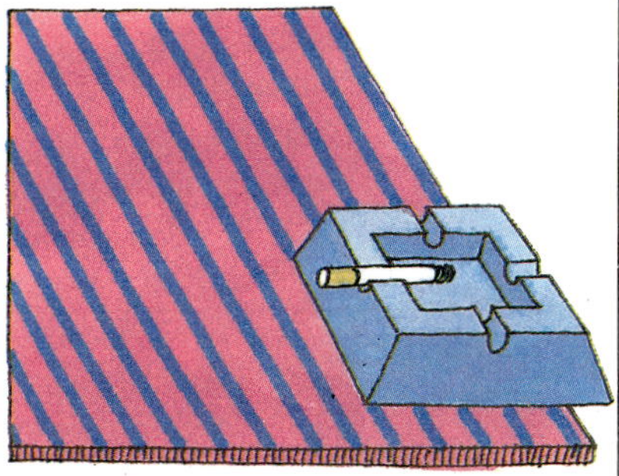

Burns: Trim burnt fibres with scissors. Then use carpet shampoo plus 1 teaspoon/5 ml white vinegar (Method 4). Rinse. Blot. Consult professionals for extensive burns and burns on synthetic fibre carpets.
Candle wax: **1** Remove deposit. **2** Place blotting paper over (and under if possible) carpet. Press with warm iron. Repeat until wax is absorbed. Change paper often. **3** Remove colour traces with methylated spirit (Method 1).
Crayon: Use dry-cleaner or lighter fuel (Method 1).

Droppings: See Vomit.
Dyes: Use methylated spirit plus a few drops of ammonia (Method 1). Test first.

Flower stains: See Grass.
Glue: See Adhesives (p. 24). If stains are indelible, trim carpet with scissors.
Grass: **1** Use methylated spirit (Method 1). **2** Use carpet shampoo (Method 4).

Grease: **1** Remove deposit. **2** Use dry-cleaner (Method 1). *Or* use iron and blotting paper, see Candle Wax. **3** Use carpet shampoo (Method 4).
Hair oil/cream: See Grease.
Ink, ballpoint: Use methylated spirit plus a little white vinegar (Method 1). *Or* use vinegar and milk (Method 4). Blot. Then see Fountain Pen Ink.
Ink, fountain pen: **1** Flush with soda syphon. Blot. **2** Use white vinegar (50:50) solution with water (Method 4). Blot. **3** Use carpet shampoo. **4** If necessary consult professionals or ink manufacturer.
Metal polish: **1** Remove deposit. **2** Use white spirit (Method 1). **3** Shampoo.

Mud: **1** Vacuum when dry. **2** Use carpet spotting kit or shampoo (Method 4). **3** Use methylated spirit (Method 1) on remaining colour.
Nail varnish: **1** Remove deposit. **2** Use amyl acetate or non-oily nail polish remover (Method 1). Test first. **3** Then use carpet shampoo (Method 4).
Oil: See Grease.

Paint: **1** Remove deposit. **2** Use dry-cleaner (Method 1). **3** Use carpet shampoo (Method 4).
Paraffin oil: See Grease. Have large areas professionally cleaned.
Plasticine: See Plasticine (p. 25).
Rust: Use rust remover. Follow instructions. Shampoo if necessary (Method 4).
Scorch marks: See Burns.

Shoe polish: **1** Remove deposit. **2** Use aerosol dry-cleaner or white spirit (Method 1). **3** If necessary, use methylated spirit (Method 1). **4** Shampoo.

Soot: **1** Vacuum carefully. **2** Use aerosol dry-cleaner (Method 1). **3** Shampoo (Method 4). Have large areas professionally cleaned.
Tar: **1** Remove deposit. **2** Rub with glycerine solution. Rinse. Blot. **3** Use dry-cleaner (Method 1). **4** If necessary rub with eucalyptus oil or paint brush cleaner (Method 1). **5** Shampoo (Method 4).
Urine: **1** Flush with soda syphon or sponge with white vinegar solution (Method 4). Blot. **2** Shampoo with added antiseptic (Method 4).
Vomit: **1** Remove deposit. **2** Flush with soda syphon. Blot. *Or* sponge with borax solution (Method 4). **3** Shampoo with added antiseptic.

Water: Mop up immediately. Dry outside if possible or artificially, raising the carpet from the floor. If flooded, call professional carpet cleaner.

Always refer to First aid and Cleaning methods (pp. 20-21) before taking action.

Alcohol: **1** Blot. **2** Squirt with soda syphon or sponge with warm water (Method 4). **3** Shampoo. **4** If necessary, rub with glycerine solution. Rinse. Dried stains: Use methylated spirit (Method 1).

Beer: **1** Flush with soda syphon or warm water (Method 4). Blot. **2** If necessary use carpet shampoo or spotting kit (Method 4). **3** Sponge old stains with methylated spirit (Method 1).

Beetroot: See Fruit.

Butter: See Grease (p. 29).

Chewing gum: See Chewing gum (p. 22).

Chocolate: **1** Remove deposit. **2** Use carpet shampoo (Method 4). Rinse. Blot dry. **3** If necessary, use liquid dry-cleaner (Method 1).

Chutney: See Jam.

Cocoa: See Chocolate. **Dried stains:** Sponge with borax solution (Method 4). Blot. **3** If necessary, rub with glycerine solution.

Coffee: **1** Blot. **2** Flush with soda syphon or cold water (Method 4). Blot. **3** If necessary use carpet shampoo or spotting kit (Method 4). **4** When dry, remove traces with dry-cleaner (Method 1).

Cream: Remove deposit. Use dry-cleaner (Method 1).

Curry: **1** Remove deposit. **2** Rub with borax solution (Method 4). *Or* rub with glycerine solution. Rinse. Blot. Have large stains professionally cleaned.

Egg: Remove deposit. Use liquid dry-cleaner (Method 1). *Or* carpet shampoo if necessary (Method 4).

Fats: See Grease (p. 29).

Fruit and fruit juices: **1** Remove deposit or blot. **2** Use carpet shampoo (Method 4). **3** If necessary use methylated spirit (Method 1). *Or* carpet spotting kit (Method 4).

Gravy: **1** Remove deposit. Blot. **2** Use liquid dry-cleaner (Method 1). **3** Use carpet shampoo (Method 4).

Honey: **1** Remove deposit. **2** Use dry-cleaner (Method 1). **3** Shampoo if necessary (Method 4).

Ice cream: **1** Remove deposit. **2** Wipe with damp cloth. **3** Use carpet shampoo (Method 4). **4** If necessary use dry-cleaner (Method 1).

Jam/marmalade: **1** Remove deposit. **2** Use carpet shampoo (Method 4). **3** If necessary, use methylated spirit (Method 1).

Juice: See Fruit.

Ketchup/bottled sauces: **1** Remove deposit. **2** Sponge with warm water or carpet shampoo (Method 4). **3** If necessary use dry-cleaner (Method 1). **Dried stains:** Rub with glycerine solution before shampooing.

Margarine: See Grease.

Mayonnaise: See Cream.

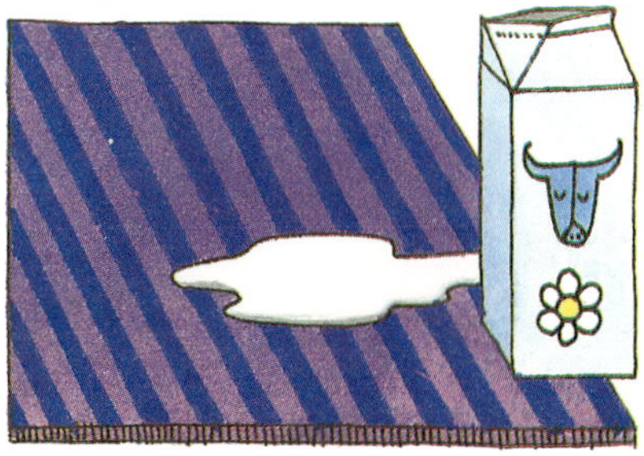

Milk: **1** Flush with soda syphon or warm water (Method 4). Blot. **2** Use carpet shampoo or spotting kit (Method 4). **3** If necessary use dry-cleaner (Method 1).

Salad dressing: See Grease.

Salt: Vacuum well.

Sauces: See Cream.

Soft drinks: See Fruit.

Soup: See Ketchup.

Spirits: See Alcohol.

Syrup: See Jam.

Tea: See Coffee. **Dried stains:** Use borax solution (Method 4).

Tomato juice: See Fruit.

Treacle: See Jam.

Wine: Act fast. **1** Flush with soda syphon or warm water; or white wine for red stain (Method 4). Blot. **2** Shampoo. **Dried stains:** Sponge with methylated spirit (Method 1). Test first.

· **Never** use soap, soap powder or soda on carpets.

· **Always** leave carpet pile leaning in correct direction.